SABINAS KID

After receiving a four-month-old letter from his mother in which she asks for his help, Caleb McConnell heads home to Colorado. But along the trail an attempt is made on his life, and Caleb begins to understand something of his parents' troubles. Why is someone after his folks' ranch, and who is behind it? When Caleb finally reaches Del Norte, childhood friendships are renewed, old grudges re-hashed, and guns blaze across the Rio Grande Valley as the mystery unfolds.

Books by Steve Ritchie
in the Linford Western Library:

THE BLACK MOUNTAIN DUTCHMAN

STEVE RITCHIE

SABINAS KID

Complete and Unabridged

LINFORD
Leicester

First published in Great Britain in 2011 by
Robert Hale Limited
London

First Linford Edition
published 2013
by arrangement with
Robert Hale Limited
London

A catalogue record for this book is available
from the British Library.

ISBN 978–1–4448–1672–3

Published by
F. A. Thorpe (Publishing)
Anstey, Leicestershire

Set by Words & Graphics Ltd.
Anstey, Leicestershire
Printed and bound in Great Britain by
T. J. International Ltd., Padstow, Cornwall

This book is printed on acid-free paper

For her patience and loving support, I dedicate this to my wife Laveina

1

Caleb McConnell wanted desperately to move, but the pain in his leg, the throbbing in his head, and the utter weakness he felt forced him to lie still. Even over the pain of his injuries, he could feel the intense, searing heat of the high desert sun on his face, as it extracted the vital moisture from his body.

He forced himself to roll his head slightly to one side, finding a weathered, bleached, buffalo skull, lying near a clump of prickly pear, just a few feet away. As he lay there looking at the stark white sign of days gone by, a desert rattler eased its way inside, through one eye of the skull, to shade itself from the sun's blistering rays.

Finally, as the sweat flowed in muddy rivulets down the sides of his dust-covered face, he was able to slowly raise a trembling hand to his head, first feeling the matted, blood-soaked hair above his right ear, and then discovering the already dried-over gash along the side of his head. Touching the wound itself caused only a little pain, but there was that crippling pounding inside his skull. Nausea engulfed him like waves of the breaking surf, causing him to vomit violently. Then, mercifully, he passed out again.

'Easy does 'er, friend,' came the words from out of the blackness of unconsciousness. Was the voice real, or was it simply a dream or the result of delirium? Caleb wasn't certain, but if it was a figment of his imagination, it was a good one, because suddenly, he felt the cool dampness of a wet cloth dabbing at the dried blood on the side of his head.

'You're hurt some, pardner. Your wounds ain't all that bad, but we gotta get some water in ya,' the voice went on. 'Here, take a swallow or two of this,' and suddenly there was the cool, refreshing presence of water on his lips.

The owner of the voice allowed him but a small amount of the wonderful fluid, but it was enough to cool his thick, parched tongue, before he again drifted back into the darkness of unconsciousness.

When Caleb again opened his sun-burned eyelids, darkness was all around him, with only the faint glimmer of the twinkling stars to convince him he was not dead, but instead still very much alive. The air was filled with the aroma of burning honey mesquite, the smoke trailing away from the small fire only a few feet away.

Again, he raised his hand to the wound above his right ear, only to discover it had been bathed and covered with some sort of salve; he assumed the salve was made by grinding the pulp of a yucca plant. His sunburned hands and face had also been covered with the same soothing paste, and it felt refreshingly cool in the night air of the Llano.

His mind was clearing, and was filled with questions for which he had no answers. It was obvious what had happened to him; he had been shot . . . ambushed. But who had done the shooting, and who was the man whose voice had come to him out of the dark fog of semi-consciousness? How badly was he injured, and where exactly was he now?

Caleb's head still throbbed and his neck was stiff, obviously from the shock of the blow to his head. He attempted to sit upright, but was much too weak. Instead, he moved his left hand to the ground and pushed with all the strength he could muster. It took a considerable effort, but finally he rolled on to his right side, which enabled him to look into the fire and survey his surroundings.

'Well, I reckon you're gonna live, friend,' came the voice again.

Looking past the fire, to the edge of the lighted area of the camp, Caleb found the source of the voice. He was nearly six feet in height and weighed, Caleb guessed, one eighty-five or so, and from the look of him, he was no pilgrim. It was difficult to make him out in the dim light of the small fire, but as he looked up at this man, the fellow's lips formed a friendly smile around the curved stem of a Mershon pipe.

'Roman Bonner's the name. I's comin' up on this waterhole from the south and saw the buzzards circlin' . I's afraid the water had gone bad or dried up, and figured to find some pilgrim all stretched out bleachin' in the sun; I's a bit worried. I have to admit to ya, friend, when I saw your layin' out here had nothin' to do with the water, I's mighty relieved.

'Now then . . . I caught a sage hen this evenin' and made some broth. Do ya feel like sittin' up for a spell and havin' a cupful?'

Caleb was weak from the loss of blood and dehydration, and wanted nothing more than to roll back to his original position and sleep. But he knew he must take on as much fluid as he could, and the broth sounded good. 'Thank ya, I'd be obliged. My belly's rubbin' a blister on my backbone; any of the meat left in that pot?'

Roman chuckled, but said nothing. After assisting Caleb in sitting upright and propping him up with his saddle, he filled a tin cup from a pan near the fire, handed it to the young man, then returned to his place at the edge of the light.

Caleb tasted the broth and it was good, salty and heavily peppered. He wanted to guzzle the tasty brew given him by this stranger, but knew he must consume it slowly. He had been injured and was severely dehydrated, but to eat or drink too much, too swiftly, would only cause him more difficulty.

Neither man spoke while Caleb sipped away at the broth. Finally, holding the cup with both hands, Caleb looked across the fire to his companion. 'Travelin' far?'

'Comin' up from Big Springs, headed

north to catch the train . . . then on home.' The big man offered no more information.

Under the small lean-to Roman had constructed by covering a crude frame of sagebrush branches with a ground sheet, Caleb sipped away at the warm broth, consuming nearly two cupfuls, before allowing his Good Samaritan to assist him as he again stretched out on the blanket beneath him. 'How long was I out?'

'Today was the third full day; I found ya a couple of hours b'fore sundown, four days ago. Looked to me like, by the blood you'd lost, you'd been there quite a spell. I estimated you'd been there since, at least, the evening before. I wasn't sure you'd make it that first night and most of that next day; you's in durn bad shape and came close to cashin' in.

'Your wounds weren't all that bad, but you'd lost a considerable amount of blood. I's able to stop your leg and side from bleedin' , that first evenin' , and to get a few swallows of water down ya, but that was about it. Layin' out there, bakin' in the sun, was your biggest problem.'

Caleb had noticed a tightness in his left leg, and now that Roman mentioned a leg wound, he moved his hand along the outside of his thigh, finding his breeches torn and a place where the skin had been stitched together; it was only slightly painful to the touch. The wound in his left side was, to his standard, a mere scratch.

'You've got another sewn up wound just like that one on the backside of that leg. Slug didn't break a bone or hit an artery, but ya still bled plenty. It passed through your leg and into your horse; I found her layin' out there, stripped of your rig.

'You dang near made it to this waterhole; got within a couple hundred yards of it. At first, I figured it was Indians bushwacked ya, there bein' huntin' parties scattered about lookin' for game around these *playas*. But since you still had possession of your hair and clothes, I decided it was somebody else did the shootin' .

'So, I had a look around and located fresh tracks of four shod horses and boot prints of three men, in a shallow wash a quarter of a mile from where I found ya. Those folks had been waitin' for quite a spell by the look of the sign they left; lots of cigarette butts, several empty tins and the like. They'd run a cold camp, but they'd been there at least a day and maybe more. You've got enemies about . . . say, friend, I didn't catch your name.'

'McConnell . . . Caleb McConnell. I'm headed fer home, too . . . Colorado. Folks got a spread up along the west face of the Cochetopa Range northwest of Del Norte.'

'Well, Caleb McConnell, there's more than enough water in this little hole to do us, so we'll stay put for a while, get ya healed up a mite, then see if we can't get ya on your way.

'For now, though, sleep's the best

medicine for ya, I think. Sleep and that broth.' Roman stretched out on his soogan, then added, 'You can sleep sound, Caleb McConnell. Ole Blue there'll let me know if we have any company,' pointing in the direction of the tall blue roan, picketed just outside the ring of light.

2

So, Caleb slept. For the next three days, he slept in the shade of the lean-to and drank more broth; one pot was made by boiling jerked beef and another from a second sage hen, caught in one of Roman's snares. On the fourth day, he was finally given a few small bites of the meat from the pot.

For another week Caleb rested, while his body healed and he regained enough strength to travel. Then on the morning of the twelfth day, after being ambushed, Roman assisted him into the saddle and led Blue and his packhorse away, west by northwest, toward the Goodnight Trail and old Fort Sumner.

Although Caleb's wounds had mended and were healing quite satisfactorily, he was still weak and tired quickly. So they traveled slowly, Roman leading the big roan and packhorse as he walked over the open ground of the Llano Estacado, or Staked Plains as they were commonly known. Early afternoon of their third day of travel found them at the plain's western rim, the Mescalero Escarpment, overlooking the Pecos River.

After locating a well-used game trail, they carefully descended the nearly three-hundred feet to the river bottom below. There Roman spread their blankets in a small cottonwood grove along the river, a place where smoke from their fire would be broken up by the foliage overhead.

Exhausted by the strenuous descent of the Mescalero Escarpment, Caleb almost immediately fell asleep. Roman allowed him to rest, while he hunted along the river for fresh meat and eatable roots. It was dark when the young man awoke to the aroma of venison roasting over a fire made of dry mesquite and pecan.

For the next two days, Roman made fried bread using flour from his packs and ground mesquite beans, allowing the young man to rest and consume as much of the roasted meat, wild vegetables and bread as he desired.

During all of those days together as they crossed the Llano, neither man had talked of himself. Each man was curious about his traveling companion, but western men did not ask questions of others. If a man wanted folks to know about his past, he voluntarily revealed what he wanted known.

But on that first night in their camp on the Pecos, Caleb opened up to Roman. They were eating quietly, enjoying the roasted venison and vegetables, the stillness of the night only being broken by the faint crackling of the fire.

Caleb began by saying, 'I call them Mom and Dad, because Mom thinks it's a show of disrespect for a fella to call his folks Maw and Paw. Anyway, my dad's an educated man. He studied geology and archeology at Cambridge University, over across the big water, teachin' there for a couple of years after finishin' his studies; that's when he met my mother.

'She was a student of his, and Dad says she's brilliant, and a much better archeologist than he. She has a portrait of the two of them on their wedding day; she was beautiful, and they made a mighty handsome couple.

'Then he was offered a job doing some digging in some ancient ruins, somewhere down in Egypt and Persia. I've been to school, when we lived in Missouri, and Mom and Dad have both schooled me after we moved to Colorado. They've shown me maps of the places they went, but I've never been to any of them.

'Anyway, they spent several years on those diggings, finding a great number of artifacts, with Dad keepin' a journal of the work they did there. The journal was published in England, after they got back, with some of those folks there at Cambridge using it to teach their students how to dig properly, what to look for and the like.'

Roman listened quietly, allowing his companion to reveal all he was willing to disclose. So far, he had heard nothing that told him how this intelligent young man had come to be a wandering cowhand and someone with enemies who would want him dead.

Caleb was educated. When they had first met, the young man spoke in the vernacular of the West, dropping the 'g' from many of his words, and using slang commonly heard in Texas and New Mexico. But now, telling his story as he relaxed over his coffee, his use of the English language was more refined, the habit of using western terminology giving way to his education.

'They finally made their way to the States, both of them teaching school in New York for a time, while they saved enough money to travel west. Then a couple of years go by and someone finds gold in the Pikes Peak country, and Dad goes to work as a geologist for a mining company. He works for those folks for a year or so, but they decide he's no longer needed and he ends up back in St. Louis, again teaching in a college.

'I came along during their first year in St. Louis, so they stayed there, wanting me to have the things a boy needs to grow up properly — a home, food on the table, and an education.'

Roman wanted to hear more about this young cowhand, so he remained quiet. He hoped he could learn something of what caused this educated youngster to abandon his civilized way of life for the rough and dangerous life of punching cows. He wanted to see what made this young man tick.

'Then, outta the blue, Dad filed on a homestead in the mountains near Del Norte. I was only nine at the time, but I recall him and Mom speaking in low tones several times, after I'd gone to bed. At the time, I didn't think she wanted to leave St. Louis. Oh, there was never any quarreling or anything like that, but I think she wanted to stay there, probably on my account.

'But we left there, Dad buying a few head of breeding stock and starting a small ranch along Cochetopa Creek north of Wagon Wheel Pass. He hired a Mexican *vaquero* to help around the place, and for a few years it looked like all was well.

'Mom got into the hang of ranch life, keeping the cabin immaculately clean, planting flowers around the place, keeping chickens — all the things a woman around a cattle outfit does to make a home in wild country, away from other folks.

'Then something happened, and I'm still not clear on what or why. Dad started paying less and less attention to the ranch, wandering off into the mountains more and more frequently. More often than not, he ignored things that needed done around the ranch, leaving it for Angel and me to attend to the cattle and to the upkeep of the place. I was going on fourteen, by then, so I was able to do my share; I suppose Dad realized that, too.

17

'Well, he would stay gone for several days at a time, going off deeper into the mountains, exploring or prospecting or whatever it was he was doing. Mom seemed to ignore the fact he was always gone, and that Angel and I were doing all the work. But to my knowledge, she never complained to Dad about it.

'Finally, one day he came home driving a herd of sheep, claiming they'd be easier to watch over than the cattle. He said he'd been to Denver, sold our herd and bought those wooly . . . critters, and that a Mexican couple, Carlos and Consuelo Urbania, came with the deal. They were going to 'help' Angel and me look after the sheep.

'Well, Angel quit on the spot and, when he left, I rode along with him. Mom cried so, I thought she'd die right then and there. I told her I simply couldn't go on watching Dad allow the place to run down to nothing. Told her I hated the smell of those sheep, and wouldn't stay there

18

and tend them. I's sixteen at the time.'

As he spoke, Caleb stared into the fire, turning his cup in his hands as he did so. Roman could see the anguish within the young man, and he felt sympathy for him.

'I bummed around for that first year, taking on one riding job after the other. I was up and down the trail a couple of times, with one cow outfit or another, first one from down around Browns-ville, then with one from south of Fort Davis.

'I was down around Fort Bliss, after that second drive, when I met Señor Zaragoza from down Nueva Rosita way. He offered me a riding job, and I took it. I've been down there for over two years.

'A week before you found me, I got a letter from my mother, telling me they had troubles. She wrote she wished I'd come home, hoping I could do something to help.

'That letter took nearly four months

19

to find me, going first to Brownsville, then to Fort Davis. Someone there must have known where I was, so they found somebody who was riding our way and sent the letter along.

'I don't know what their trouble is, but I've got to get home. Mom wouldn't have sent for me, if they weren't in dire need of help.'

Now, he tipped his cup, finishing his coffee. Then, without saying another word, he rolled into his blankets. Roman stared at the bulk lying near the fire. He very much liked this youngster, and wished he could help him and his parents.

But Roman Bonner had a job of his own to do. The information he had obtained recently was an important clue in finding the man he pursued. Well, he had saved Caleb's life and was happy he had been able to help him as much as he had.

3

Finally leaving their camp on the Pecos and following the river north for several days, they reached Pete Maxwell's ranch near Fort Sumner, a place where Roman was known. There, Roman made arrangements with Maxwell for a horse for Caleb, and for enough supplies to see the young puncher to his home and family.

Caleb was a good-natured, friendly young man, making friends quickly with his easy-going, pleasant manner. So, there at the Maxwell ranch, he rested for another week and continued to regain his strength, talking and laughing with the Maxwells and their hired help, but resting often. By the end of the week, Caleb was able to walk the ranch yard without the aid of the cane Roman had whittled from a mesquite branch, and he was antsy, tired of loafing around and eager to get out and about.

From time to time during that week, Roman loitered in the saloons in the settlement near the old fort, picking up bits and pieces of interesting information regarding several subjects of interest to him. Twice he sent telegrams, which included some of the information he'd gained, to his office in Kansas City.

On the afternoon of their last day in Sumner, Roman was loafing, and nursing a rare, cool beer, at a table in the back of the Bosque Redondo Saloon. There were five other men there; two old men playing a game of checkers near a window in the front, the others were men in their twenties, who drank at a table along the far wall from where he sat. By their dress one would think they were ordinary cowhands, but each sported a pair of tied-down six-guns.

Roman was simply relaxing, thinking about preparations he must make to resume his journey, when Caleb ambled through the batwing doors and, revealing a slight limp, made his way toward the bar. Around his waist hung a well worn gunbelt.

When Caleb entered the saloon, he glanced first to his right, saw Roman, nodded and flashed his friend a wide grin; he failed to look to his left. As he approached the bar, he called out to the barkeep, ordering his beer, and drew the attention of the three men seated across the room.

Roman noticed the immediate change in their disposition, at seeing his young friend. Instinctively, he put two and two together, recognizing the sign of men surprised to see someone, someone whom they thought dead.

Cold beer is a rare thing in the south-west, especially where Caleb had been working in Mexico, a country where ice is not present in the summer months. But here at the fort, ice was brought from the mountains in huge blocks, from an ice cave, and kept in a limestone blockhouse. So he was looking forward to a cool glass, knowing the kegs were kept in that ice house.

'How ya doin' , Kid?' asked one of the three.

Caleb was reaching for the glass of beer, which the bartender had already placed on the bar, but stopped short when he heard the voice. Without saying a word, Roman downed the amber liquid remaining in his glass, rose from his chair, then walked nonchalantly to the bar near Caleb. There he placed the empty glass on the plank that served as the bar and motioned to the bartender for a refill. Caleb's eyes caught his movements.

As he lifted the glass of beer with his right hand, Caleb slowly turned to face the three men, all of whom were rising to their feet.

'I'm good, Dieter. How 'bout you boys? A bit far off your range, ain't ya?'

Dieter Metzger shrugged. 'I don't reckon I've been fenced in nowheres, yet. My range is wherever I'm ridin' .'

Caleb put the glass to his lips and tipped it, taking several swallows, consuming more than half of the cool liquid. Then he placed the glass back on the bar, as Roman eased his hand inside his coat, placing it on the grips of the short-barreled Schofield .45 that hung there.

'Kid, it must be true what they say, 'bout you bein' part cat, with nine lives and all,' Metzger sneered. 'I surely figured we done fer ya, out yonder on the Llano. Reckon three weren't enough . . . shoulda weighted ya down.'

'Looks like it . . . but for sure, you shoulda started shootin' b'fore I set that glass down; you'd at least have had a chance then. Now . . . ya got none a-tall.'

He'd barely finished speaking, when, as one man, the three reached for iron. Suddenly, flames darted from the muzzles of five six-guns and the room echoed with the sound of what seemed like crashing thunder, as it filled with the acidulous smell of burnt powder.

Roman, Schofield in hand, joined Caleb, who was punching empties from his Navy Colt, as he glared at the three bodies on the floor. 'Dang, Caleb! I take it ya knew those ole boys?'

'Yep. Soon as I seen them three, I knew they's the ones who shot me out yonder. Dieter Metzger and the Bauer brothers, Adrian and Conrad . . . they all come from over east of here in the Texas Hill Country. Dieter's folks got a farm south of the Balcones, them brothers was from over on the Guadalupe River, around Kerrville.

'Rode opposite those three in a little ruckus down west of Nueva Rosita, a year or so back. Dieter's brother, August, these three and a few other fellas were running stock off the place I's working for down on the Sabinas River. Me and two other fellas trailed 'em 'til we caught up to 'em, north of Del Rio. After a bit of a scrap, we'd done for five of their bunch, but both Metzgers, the Bauers and a couple

26

others were able to give us the slip and hightailed it north, outta the neighborhood.

'Like I said, that was more'n a year back. I ain't seen any of 'em since . . . 'til now. Mighty dang coincidental they's out on the Llano and just happened across me yonder, ain't it?'

As a crowd gathered on the porch, just outside the batwing doors, Roman examined the bodies of the three dead men. All had been punched where it counted most, and more than once. At least six shots had been fired so closely together, one could not have counted just how many there had been. But Caleb McConnell had dropped two of them, he the other, with only a single round each being fired by the Bauer brothers and Dieter Metzger. Roman found one splintered hole in the plank floor, near the feet of Conrad Bauer and two others in the far wall near where he'd sat.

'This kid is fast . . . dang fast,' Roman thought to himself.

4

Within him, Caleb felt the urgency to reach his home and bring a solution to the troubles confronting his parents. He found his outfit and money among the belongings of Metzger and the Bauer brothers. So, although Roman and the Maxwells agreed he needed a few more days to recuperate, on the day after the shooting, he threw his Mexican saddle on the back of an Overo paint, given him by Pete Maxwell, and the two men said their goodbyes to the folks at the ranch, riding away leading Roman's packhorse.

By being in the saddle before sunrise each morning and stopping to make their camp at dusk each evening, late on the third day from Fort Sumner, they walked their horses down the main street of Santa Fe. The sun had set hours before and both men, and their animals, were dog tired.

After seeing to their horses, they walked side-by-side to the beautiful Plaza Hotel, where Roman secured rooms for them. With a mariachi band playing on the bandstand across the yard, they were having their supper in the pleasant atmosphere of the hotel's open-air plaza dining area, when the town's marshal, Mike Simpson, approached their table.

'Roman, how ya been?'

'Mike. You?'

'Just fine. Things have been quiet around Santa Fe lately. That's one of the reasons I came by tonight.'

Then Simpson turned to Caleb. 'Kid, I just wanted to make sure you's movin' on in the mornin' .'

Simpson stood a good three inches over six feet and weighed two forty, a long handlebar mustache adorned his upper lip, and a pair of blue-gray eyes, that could stare a hole through a man, glared sternly from under the wide brim of his flat-crowned hat. But Caleb continued to eat while the lawman spoke, electing not to look up at the big man.

'Hold on a minute, Mike,' Roman cut in. 'We just hit town half an hour ago. Caleb here was dry-gulched a while back; suffered a couple of wounds and was in pretty bad shape for a spell. We've been doing some hard travelin' for the past few days, and he might just wanta rest a bit.'

Simpson looked at Roman queerly. 'I'm surprised a man of your position would be ridin' with an *hombre* like this, Ro. You know who this kid is?'

Roman detected the innuendo in the marshal's question. 'Well, yeah, he's Caleb McConnell,' he answered ambiguously. 'Said he's been ridin' for an outfit down in Old Mexico for the last few years, and now he's headin' to his folk's place north of Del Norte. Who do you say he is?'

Given enough time, stories circulate across the West, stories of heroic acts, tragedies, cattle drives, of gunfights and of gunfighters. Now, suddenly, something surfaced in Roman's mind . . . something that had been there from that day in the Bosque Redondo Saloon. Dieter Metzger had called him 'Kid,' not Caleb or McConnell, when he had addressed him. Now, the term 'Kid' took on a whole new meaning for Roman.

'Keep movin' , Big Man,' Caleb suddenly blurted. 'I ain't got much use for the law . . . and all I'm doin' is havin' my supper.'

'Got no use for the law — ' Simpson said, but was cut short by Roman.

'Mike, what's this all about?'

Mike Simpson had been a lawman for over twenty years, all of his adult life. He had been the local law in Eagle Pass, Texas, until he took the job in Santa Fe eighteen months before.

A few months before Simpson departed his old job, three hands from Ignacio Zaragoza's outfit, El Ranchero de Sabinas, had recovered three dozen head of short-horn steers from a bunch of thieves, led by August Metzger, and had driven them into Eagle Pass to sell; all of which was perfectly legal. Caleb McConnell had been leading the Zaragoza riders.

On their first night in town, the marshal had heard shots being fired and immediately headed for the Glass House Saloon. When he walked through the door, he found two dead men on the floor, one with his weapon lying beside him, the other still with his six-gun in its holster. He asked the first man he saw, a witness to the event, the identity of the man who had done the shooting.

'El Chico Sabinas, Señor Marshal,' the man answered, as he pointed toward a young man near the bar, the one punching empty cases from the cylinder of his converted Navy Colt.

It had proven to be a fair fight, but the next morning, Simpson had learned more about the reputation of Caleb McConnell, better known as 'The Sabinas Kid'. He immediately ordered Caleb to surrender his weapons or leave town; Caleb chose to ride.

'You wanna tell him, Kid, or do ya want me to?'

'You're doin' all right, mister. B'sides, I ain't finished my supper, yet, and I don't want it to get cold.'

Simpson gave Caleb a hard look, then turned back to Roman, identifying Caleb as the Sabinas Kid and telling Roman all he knew about him.

'Now, all the witnesses, there at the Glass House, said them other two jaspers started the ruckus and reached first, but this kid didn't offer to back up none. The Kid's built himself a right smart reputation as a gunhand, Roman.'

He continued to tell other stories he had heard about Caleb, stories that had been told to him since their first meeting.

'Now I'll admit, most all them stories I heard was about him lookin' out for Ole Man Zaragoza. If somebody down yonder caused that ole man grief, runnin' off cattle or tryin' to squat on a piece of his grazin' land, McConnell here took care of things.

'My main problem with all I heard, was that The Kid never brought back any survivors . . . they's always diggin' graves b'hind him.'

Roman was nodding as Simpson told his story, and the marshal had been right, it probably wouldn't look so good for him to be riding with someone who had such a reputation. However, Roman Bonner rarely concerned himself with public opinion.

'Well, Mike, I'm staying here until the east-bound train comes through; I'll be takin' it on home. As far as Caleb here is concerned, I'll take responsibility for his actions, while he's in town. You won't have any trouble from us.'

Mike Simpson peered thoughtfully at the man who sat across the table from Caleb. He had known Roman Bonner for many years, having had a number of occasions to work with the man.

'OK, Roman. If you say so, I'll let him stay. But he leaves his sidearms in his room as long as he's here . . . and that ain't negotiable. When you go, he goes.'

Roman looked across the table at his young companion; Caleb was looking back at him. To say the least, Caleb was reluctant to be seen 'naked' in public. But Roman was willing to stand up to this lawman for him, and there was little chance he would have any problems here in Santa Fe, anyway. One short nod was his response to Roman.

'All right, Mike. We'll do it your way.'

So Marshal Mike Simpson exited the courtyard, going about his duties. Roman and Caleb finished their meal, then Caleb took his sidearms to his room. When he returned to the hotel lobby, the two men retired to the adjoining cantina, where they enjoyed a few glasses of cold beer and pleasant conversation. After a while, they joined three other gentlemen in a low stakes game of draw poker.

With his winnings in his pocket, two days after their conversation with

Marshal Simpson, Caleb pulled stakes for Del Norte. Roman caught the train for Kansas City the following morning. He did not ask Caleb any questions concerning his former employment, or his reputation.

5

Caleb rode north along the western face of the Sangre de Cristo Range, crossing the Rio Grande midday of the second day to travel an ancient game trail, just below the treeline along the east face of the San Juans. The trail had seen little or no use for some time, giving him to believe he could travel unobserved by using this route.

Several times he saw elk and deer. Twice he found fresh tracks of grizzlies, one of which had been eating only a hundred yards down the mountainside below the trail. The great bear had stood on his hind legs and watched him as he passed by, testing the air and growling in a low tone. Caleb kept his Winchester across the pommel, ready to use if the brute decided to attack.

Late afternoon of the third day, he rode down off the mountain and crossed the river north of Taos, once more finding a game trail along the face of the Sangre de Cristos. The sun was setting below the peaks of the San Juans when he followed Vallajo Creek down the mountain to the edge of San Pablo, a small *pueblo* built along the banks of Ventero Creek.

Circling the tiny *pueblo*, he finally stepped down in front of a lovely adobe that was encircled by a vine-covered wall, four-feet high. Tying a line to the ring on the hitching post near the gate, Caleb stepped through the opening in the short adobe wall, pulled the rope on the small bell, which hung overhead, then took a step back away from the door.

The woman who answered the bell carried an oil lamp. When the light from that lamp touched the face of the man who had rung the bell, her dark eyes grew large and her mouth opened wide, as she gasped with delight.

'Oh, *Dios mío*! Señor Caleb! Come in, come in.' Then she turned away and hurried toward the great room. 'Manuel, is Caleb! Come Manuel!'

Caleb could not help but chuckle as he removed his sombrero and entered the house. Margarita was the sister of Angel Hernandez, the *vaquero* who had ridden for his father. So, whenever he and Angel had ridden this way, they had always stopped here at the home of Manuel and Margarita Gomez. They had always made him feel welcome, and this time was going to be no exception.

Manuel, who had been eating his supper, rushed in from the kitchen and grabbed his hand, shaking it violently as he clapped him on the back.

'Señor Caleb, it is very good to see you, *mi amigo*. How are you? Have you been well? It has been such a very long time since we have seen you.' Manuel's black eyes gleamed at seeing his young friend, and he spoke so rapidly Caleb hadn't time to answer his questions. 'Come to the kitchen. Eat with us and tell us what you do all this time. You have grown so tall, my young friend, but otherwise, you have changed little. Come.' So Caleb followed his friend to the table and found himself a chair.

Manuel was not a tall man, standing only five feet seven inches, weighing one hundred forty pounds, ruggedly handsome with his long black hair and mustache. He sat a horse, as any *vaquero* Caleb had ever observed, as if he were an extension of the animal.

Margarita was a beautiful woman, nearly as tall as her husband, one hundred twenty pounds, with a curvaceous body, jet black hair and eyes that looked like deep pools of oil.

His hostess placed a plate of sliced beef, beans, and rice before him, along with a cup of steaming hot coffee. From a plate in the center of the table he retrieved a tortilla, spread butter on it, then forked up a mouthful of the beef.

They wanted to know all that had happened over the past three years, where he had gone, how he had made his living and so on. So he answered their questions, giving them only the details he wanted them to know, leaving out all of the events involving gunplay and his reputation.

Once they had the answers to their questions, he asked, 'How have y'all been? And what's Angel up to these days?'

Manuel was saddened. 'Angel is dead, Caleb.'

'Dead? How on earth did that happen?'

Slowly, regretfully Manuel explained. 'He rides for a man in Arizona. His horse falls in a stampede and Angel is trampled. That happens last summer.'

Well, Angel was gone. He had not only been Caleb's friend and companion, but his mentor. He had taught Caleb all the boy knew of cattle, horses, and even of men. 'Trust few men, *chico*,' Angel had said. 'One can count his *true* friends on one hand. Always be honest and trustworthy, but trust with caution those whom you must rely upon.'

It hadn't made a lot of sense to the

young boy who had ridden daily with the *vaquero*. But once he was on his own, Caleb had learned quickly the meaning of Angel's teaching. He had become wary of strangers and eventually grew to trust no one, with only one exception, Ignacio Zaragoza . . . and he *never* relied upon anyone for help, no matter what the situation.

So, they ate and they talked. Finally Caleb asked if they had had any word of his parents.

'*Sí*, Caleb, we have heard they have trouble,' Manuel stated. 'I am not certain what their troubles are, but the man who tells me this said there is much talk of serious trouble on Cochetopa Creek.'

What sort of trouble could they have gotten into? His parents had lived there for over ten years and had not crossed anyone's lines or infringed on any other rancher's graze. Not many cattlemen would tolerate sheep on the range, but there was more than enough grass in that valley up there, and besides, those sheep mostly grazed on the grass along the slopes of the mountains.

But that was the only thing that made sense. One of the neighboring ranchers, or all of them, wanted those devilish sheep off the range. Well, Caleb couldn't blame them for that, for he hated the wooly varmints, too. 'When I get there, I'll put an end to their trouble in a hurry,' he thought.

Supper was over and Caleb and Manuel smoked quietly, while seated in heavily padded armchairs before the fireplace. When Margarita finished washing the dishes, she joined them for a while, all enjoying the fire as they talked. Finally the hour grew late and she showed Caleb to his room.

He had spent many nights in this room as a boy, Angel sleeping there next to him. But now his old friend was gone and he was a grown man — of nineteen — and it would be up to him to protect the Rafter MC Ranch. If the ranches that bordered his parents' spread were looking for trouble, he was just the man who could take it to them.

6

Margarita insisted on feeding Caleb, before he left for Del Norte. So, after having his beefsteak and eggs, he saddled the paint and stepped up. Manuel insisted he send for him if he needed help. Caleb smiled at his friend and nodded, then reined his horse to the northwest and nudged him with a heel.

Crossing the floor of the valley, he made his way back to the river, which he crossed once more, continuing across the valley to Raton Creek. Following the creek up the mountain, he rode up the aspen and pine-covered slope coming to its headwaters and the narrow pass between Horse and Dog Mountains.

Riding through the pass he found another trail, one that wound its way along the southwestern slope of Dog

Mountain. Here was another well-marked, ancient trail, of which there were many in these mountains, that had long been used by Indians as they moved between their summer camps in Wyoming and Montana to their wintering grounds to the south.

Caleb loved this wild country; he had long believed he had been born for it. He loved the smell of the pines, the pungent fragrance of the sagebrush mixed with the sweetness of the wild flowers, which were so plentiful.

In the meadows and along the mountainside, where a recent fire had burned a magnificent stand of aspens, the blossoms of the Fireweed, Yellow Paintbrush, Mertensia and Columbine blanketed the ground, adding a burst of color that nearly took his breath away.

Twice he stopped at streams allowing the paint to drink. He crossed back over the mountain to the northern slope and nooned along San Francisco Creek, where he ate the food Margarita Gomez had insisted he take; slices of beef wrapped in tortillas.

When he reached Piños Creek, the sun was setting. As the cloak of darkness now obscured the timber-covered slope, he turned north, following the creek down the mountain, then along its east fork to the place where it joined the west fork a couple of miles south of the Rio Grande. There he left its banks.

The lights of Del Norte showed dimly in the distance. Caleb rode those last two miles with care, the tension building within him. There was trouble up ahead, trouble he had nearly no knowledge of. He would stop at the Cantina Rio to see what information he could pick up, then light out for the ranch, spending the night somewhere along the trail.

He walked the paint along the southern edge of town, along the back of the buildings that bordered First Street, until he turned up the alley between Conrad's Mercantile and Daniel Hodge's law office.

Walking the length of the alley, Caleb

stopped in the shadow of Conrad's store and sat the weary paint, listening. Off to his right, he could hear the tinny music, coming from the piano inside Elmer Grant's Big Bear Saloon, as Homer Ludlow tickled the ivories; Homer had been playing that same old beat-up piano for as long as Caleb could remember. Amanda Sterling was singing along with the music . . . and she could sing. With a voice as sweet as a nightingale, she sang the chorus of The Vacant Chair.

'She'll have 'em cryin' in their beer, b'fore she's finished,' he mumbled, as he chuckled and nudged the paint again.

Having surveyed the street and found it empty, he eased across First Street, entering the alley on the other side, finally stopping before stepping out on to Front Street.

Finally, turning west on Front Street, Caleb walked his horse up to Cedar Street, reined the paint to his right, and rode up to The Rio; still he had seen no one. With the exception of the Big Bear, the whole town was unusually quiet and seemed deserted.

At the Cantina Rio he stepped down, slipped a line around the rail and tied it in a slip knot, then loosened the cinch, his eyes taking in his surroundings as he did so.

During his ride north from Santa Fe, he had given much thought to his attackers, there on the Llano Estacado. The Llano is a vast, rolling expanse, and rarely, if ever, does a man come upon other riders as he travels across it. But those three had been there at the very waterhole at which he had planned to stop. That could not have been a coincidence.

But it appeared that, somehow, they had known he had been sent for by his mother and had waited for him there. Roman had said the signs pointed to their having been concealed there at least a day, and he suspected it had been closer to three.

Three days they had waited in hiding

. . . waited for *him*. Why? And how did they find out he was coming north? How did they guess he would be coming along that particular route? Was their being there connected with the troubles his folks were having? If so, how did they get involved and who was behind it all? All questions he must find the answers to.

He stepped up on to the boardwalk and hitched his guns into position, slipping the thongs from the hammers of both. He was ready to step through the door, when suddenly a voice came from the shadows, calling out to him from off to his right.

'Caleb? Caleb McConnell? Is that you, boy?'

Caleb immediately crouched as he turned, his Colt magically appearing in his left hand. A short, dark figure stood in the space between The Rio and Harvey Ingram's barber shop.

'Come out into the light, Hoss.'

'Fer God sakes, Caleb, don't shoot me. It's Grady Bolton, son. You remember me, don't ya?'

'Sure, Grady, I remember ya well. Come on out here where I can see ya.'

Grady Bolton was an old prospector, a wiry old man with white hair, pale blue eyes and a wrinkled sun-baked face that was, more often than not, covered by a scraggly, white beard. He had come to these mountains during the Pikes Peak gold rush, staying on all these years, even after he had failed to strike it rich. Wandering over the surrounding mountains for over twenty-five years, Grady had found a bit of color here and a bit more there, panning out just enough for a big fling once in a while, and, sometimes, enough for supplies afterward.

But he had remained poor, while others who had come at the same time had gotten rich and moved on. More than once Caleb's father had grubstaked Grady, being promised a share in whatever he found. To Caleb's knowledge, his father had never received one dime from the old man, but he kept on giving the old prospector supplies and money enough to continue on with his gold hunting.

'I reckoned that were you, Caleb, when I seen the way ya walked up them steps. Men change, as they grows older, but I'da knowed ya anywheres. How ya been, son?' But before Caleb could answer, Bolton whispered, 'Things ain't good 'round here, Caleb. No sir, not good a'tall. They's trouble up north along Cochetopa Crik. Trouble a-plenty.'

Caleb stopped the old man. 'Grady, come inside and we'll have a talk,' and he took him by the arm.

Inside, there was only one man, unknown to Caleb, who stood at the bar; behind the bar was Charlie Gantz, the barkeep. Caleb ordered coffee for himself, and a bottle and glass for Grady. Picking up the drinks from the bar, he led the old man to a table in the back corner and took a seat. As Grady downed a couple of shots from the bottle, Caleb inquired about the trouble he had spoken of.

'I ain't fer sure what's goin' on,

Caleb. Thangs been happenin' up yonder that don't make no sense.'

'You make sense, Grady. What's been happenin'?'

He took another swallow from his glass, wiped his mouth with the back of his sleeve and set the glass on the table.

'Well, it goes a fer piece back, b'fore you even lef' here.' He put the glass to his lips once more, then went on with his story. 'Back 'bout four year ago, yore pappy went to traipsin' 'round the mountains north of his ranch. I seen him as fer north as Pennsylvany Mountain and as fer east as Tater Top.' The old man was speaking loud enough for the men at the bar to hear him.

'Keep it down, Grady. Keep it low.'

'OK, son,' the old man whispered. 'OK, sorry. Anyway, I reckoned he'd got the fever an' was off lookin' fer the vein I ain't been able to locate. Reckoned he'd got tired of waitin' fer me to strike it rich an' jus' decided to go fer it his own self.

'Well, I sorta follered him 'round up

yonder oncest, just to see if'n he were makin' any headway. But I fin'lly fig'red he couldn't be lookin' fer no gold, 'cause he were lookin' in the wrong places.

'What I mean is, yore pappy is a man what knows rock formations and the like, him bein' eddicated and all. I'd tried to talk him into comin' out with me a time or two, but he never did wanna leave the ranch. Said he never reckoned to go huntin' gold. Said the big pockets was farther east, although he reckoned there'd be a small patch here an' yonder, scattered amongst these hills west of The Peak.

'But jus' watchin' him, I seen right off he weren't lookin' fer gold. I can't say, an' won't try to reckon, what it were he's after, but it weren't gold . . . not unless he were dumb as a post.

'So after you lit-out, and he had them dang sheep runnin' all up an' down the mountainside with them Mexicans watchin' after 'em, he went to takin' your maw with him on his treks. 'Bout a year back, I come across 'em camped up on Starvation Crik, in that valley b'twixed Mount Ouray and Windy Point.

'Now I done looked that country over, Caleb, and there ain't enough color in that neck-o-the-woods to pay a man a day's wage. But yore folks stayed on yonder fer nigh on to a week. I perceded on north, after spottin' 'em up yonder, an' come back that way a week later, an' they's still camped on the same spot. Didn't make no sense then an' it don't make no sense now — not to me, nohow.'

Caleb was shaking his head, because it didn't make any sense to him, either. He could not believe his father had caught the gold fever and had abandoned the ranch. Granted, he had sold the cattle and bought the sheep, but cattle prices had faltered and the price of sheep had been on a steady incline. The price of wool had been on the up swing and if that Urbania fellow, the man his father had hired to care for the flock, was any good with a pair of shears, there was probably money to be made. Knowing his father as he thought he did, he must assume the decision to get out of the cattle business and into the sheep business had been made as strictly a business move.

While Caleb was giving all the old man had said some thought, Grady took another swallow from his glass, then added, 'Now the cabin's gone, son. They's all gone.'

'What are ya talkin' about, Grady? What cabin's gone? Who's gone?'

Grady suddenly realized Caleb had not heard the news. 'Yore folk's cabin ... and that cabin of them Mexicans what worked fer 'em. Fire started up yonder in one of them cabins and, 'cause they's so closet t'gether, I reckon t'other'n catched, too, an' they both burnt to the ground. Four souls lost in that one fire.'

What was he saying? Caleb simply could not comprehend the message in the words the old man had just spoken.

'What cabins are you talkin' about, Grady?'

The old prospector could see Caleb's confusion. 'After you lef', yore pappy built them Mexicans a cabin right next to their'n. That Mex knowed sheep mighty good and that flocks growed to more'n seven hundr'd head. I reckon yore pappy had money comin' in from the wool, and he'd sold what rams he'd not needed, so I'd say he were showin' a right fare profit.

'Anyhow, they's livin' right closet t'gether yonder. Then one day a couple o' months back, I went up thataway and were gonna stop fer a visit ... I's hopin' yore maw'd invite me to supper, like she always done. When I crossed West Pass Crik and looked up on that bench where their cabins was, all I seen were the chimney of the big house.

'When I got up yonder on that bench, I seen a sight that made my blood curdle. Both them cabins was burnt plumb to the ground. Off a ways to the east, from the big cabin, was four

56

graves. Looked like somebody'd come along an' found their remains and buried 'em.' He refilled his glass, then went back to his drinking.

Caleb sat there in the Cantina Rio, shocked to the core by the news he had just been given. Suddenly, his parents were dead.

It was not uncommon for a cabin to burn down. Cinders from the chimney could ignite the cedar shingles on the roof, or a stray spark would find some material inside the house that would burn quickly. It was simply a common occurrence.

But now it had happened to his parents, and he was having a great deal of difficulty comprehending the results of this particular event.

7

When Caleb left the Cantina Rio, Grady Bolton gathered his mules and rode with him. For nearly two hours they rode through the night, clouds more often than not blotting out the moon. Finally, they pulled up along Carnero Creek and made their camp at the edge of an aspen grove at the base of the La Garita Range.

Caleb started a fire, while Grady saw to their animals, unsaddling all three and staking them close by on a good patch of grass near the creek. After having eaten their supper, Caleb took the makings from his shirt pocket, rolled a smoke and put flame to it. As he smoked and drank his coffee, he gave thought to the information given him by the old prospector, there in the cantina.

'Grady, were any of the ranchers

givin' Dad grief over bringin' sheep into the neighborhood?'

Shaking his head, Grady responded quickly. 'Nah, he weren't botherin' none of them. Their stock's got more grass an' water'n they's ever likely to need.'

Finally they pulled the bigger sticks away from the flames and allowed the fire to burn down to embers. Caleb still sat quietly smoking, running what he had been told over and over in his mind. Suddenly there was the sound of a bullet parting the air and a wicked 'whack' from an aspen that grew behind and just to his left. Both he and Grady were already diving for cover when they heard the heavy report of the rifle. As he settled himself behind a log, Caleb heard the old prospector yell out in pain.

'Grady, you hit?'

'Nah, just landed on a cactus. Caleb, that were a big-bore Sharps or the like. That fella's out yonder a few hundred yards — took a while fer the report to git here after that slug hit that tree yonder.'

Caleb could not understand why someone was trying to kill him, and now, this was the second attempt. Of course Metzger and the Bauers had lain for him out on the Llano, but they had good reason, after the episode down along the border. But here? And now?

He had been fairly certain no one had seen him enter Del Norte, but obviously, someone had. Who . . . the two men in the cantina? Why would anyone try to kill him? Who the devil was behind it all? What did all of this have to do with his parents?

Now, safely concealed behind the log on which he had been seated, Caleb rolled another smoke and put a match to it, while mulling over this current shooting. Trying to recall as best he could, he estimated that nearly two seconds elapsed between the bullet striking the tree and his hearing the report. Three to four hundred yards and the report was heavy. He was certain Grady was right — a big-bore Sharps, Remington or Ballard. These were not your everyday choice of weapons, but not all that uncommon in this country.

For another hour they lay behind their individual cover. When the embers of the fire were all but dead, each man slipped from his hiding place, making his way in the darkness to their animals.

After Caleb saddled the paint, he helped Bolton saddle and load his mules. Under the cover of the darkness among the aspen, they cautiously and quietly moved up Carnero Creek to its south fork, then followed that fork to its headwaters. From there, Caleb led the way over a low saddle to the opposite side of the mountain, then turned south-east along its face.

Now, the hour was late. The clouds were scattered and the moon shone down allowing him sufficient light to find his way along a game trail that ran along the pine and aspen-covered slope. Gradually, he descended to the banks of Little La Garita Creek below, finally turning north again.

Again the clouds gathered, streaked with several shades of pink and red by the morning sun. Caleb rode through the foothills, circling toward the place where he believed the shooter from the night before had made his shot. The only clear view, at the range from which Grady had suggested the shot had come, was from a low ridge nearly a quarter of a mile from their former campsite.

Another hour found them ascending the eastern slope of the low hill he was looking for. Just below the ridge, Caleb dismounted, removed his sombrero and hung it on the saddle-horn, then cautiously crept to the top, concealing himself behind the many clumps of sagebrush and junipers as he moved. Grady remained with the animals.

Half an hour after leaving the old man, Caleb reappeared, walking upright, heading back toward Grady. When he was back in his saddle, he rode once again up Carnero Creek past their camp of the night before, walking the paint in the creek itself.

Grady was full of questions and about to burst. 'Well? Are ya ever gonna tell me what the deuce ya found?'

Caleb had been thinking, coming up with only few answers. Now his thoughts had been interrupted by his old companion, and he had no choice but to chuckle.

'Sorry, ole timer. I reckon I was all caught up in my thoughts. Reckon I've been a lone rider for too long.

'That outcrop we passed, when we crossed over that ridge, showed signs of somebody bein' there, all right. Didn't look like he stayed long, but I'd say that's where he took his shot from. He musta cleaned up his brass, too, 'cause I didn't find any layin' around. But I'm sure that's where he set up his shootin' station.'

'Well, sir, that were nigh onta four hund'rd yards from our camp,' Grady stated. 'With what little light he had, he was bound ta used one o' them long brass sights. I'm a mite puzzled a fella with that kinda shootin' iron could miss ya, even in that low light.'

That gave Caleb even more to think about. Grady was right. Anyone who owned a weapon like that would certainly know how to shoot, and four hundred yards was no difficult shot for a Sharps or similar rifle with a telescopic sight . . . even in low light.

The clouds overhead grew heavier, hovering close to the mountains and concealing the higher peaks. Both men donned their slickers, and by mid-morning they were riding up the creek in a light, cold rain, neither man talking, riding silently and deep in his own thoughts.

When they again reached the head-waters of the middle fork of Carnero Creek, Caleb made his way through the pines down the western slope of the mountain, then rode north through California Gulch to the mouth of Grouse Creek. There they nooned under an overhang near the stream.

Caleb put a fire together under the deep rocky ledge, while the old man brought bacon and coffee from the packs on the mule. Grady filled the pot with clear, icy water from the creek, dumped in a handful of Arbuckle's, then sat it next to the fire to boil. Caleb took his bone-handled knife to the bacon and placed a half dozen thick slices in a skillet, then took out his makings. Still neither man spoke.

While their food cooked, Caleb rolled his smoke. When he had lighted it and taken a couple of deep draws, he looked toward Grady.

'How was Mom and Dad, the last time you saw them?'

Grady smiled. He knew Caleb had many things on his mind, but had been surprised he had not asked the question before now.

'Well, they was good. Like I told ya last night, your maw'd went to traipsin' 'round with your pappy out on his jaunts into them mountains. She loved that ranch an' these ole mountains, an' she never let on to me she weren't happy trekkin' 'long after him. She even said oncest it were like they's on their secon' honeymoon.'

Caleb only shook his head. He was trying to put the pieces of the puzzle together, but *nothing fit*. His mother had sent for him four months ago, telling him they had troubles and needed his help. And three men had attempted to kill him at a time and in a place where only Ignacio Zaragoza had known he would be.

There were simply too many variables involved in making a trip like that — having to avoid Indians, knowing the available waterholes where one was not likely to run into trouble, current weather conditions, and more. Even he had not been certain of his exact route, only expressing to Señor Zaragoza his possible travel plans.

The pieces simply didn't fit, and still the questions remained. Why? Who was behind it all? As Grady forked up the crisp strips of pork, Caleb's head was aching.

'What we gonna do next, son?'

Caleb smiled at the old man. 'We?'

'Why shore,' the old man said with a chuckle. 'I can see right off you can't stay outta trouble. You need somebody to watch after ya.'

What could Caleb say to that? He was a man who, while he had worked side by side with other men, preferred to work alone. Angel had taught him to trust no one for help, especially when it came to facing trouble, and over the past three years trouble had seemed to find him often.

But for now, he would allow the old man to ride with him. Perhaps there might be questions Grady could answer. He would see.

Caleb followed Grouse Creek to its headwaters, then rode over the mountain and down the other side into the Saguache Valley. Turning north once again, even in the rain they made better time, riding over the short, green grass of the valley, until they entered Mexican Gulch.

Traveling up Mexican Gulch for more than a dozen miles, they crossed the Cochetopa Range, coming out into a valley six miles wide and nine miles long, the valley of the Cochetopa Dome. This was the southern end of the ranch known as the Rafter MC.

Still riding north, it was an hour past sunset when they climbed the steep grade to the bench upon which the ranch buildings had been built. Even in the darkness and drizzle, Caleb made out the charred remains of the houses. The two barns, the crib, smokehouse and spring house still stood near by, having not been burned along with the houses. But he would need more light to look the place over.

They led their animals into the barn, stripped them of their gear, then scooped oats from a sack and forked hay from the loft. Finally, they laid their blankets upon small piles of hay, pulled from the stack and forked into the driveway.

Outside the wind blew and the rain fell in a light mist, making the relative warmth of the barn a welcome relief from the possibility of spending a night exposed to the elements.

Caleb spent a restless night, questions spinning in his head, keeping him awake for several hours after they turned in. He never noticed when the rain stopped.

8

Daylight found Grady squatting a few feet from the cabin, watching his young friend, while Caleb sifted through the ashes and charred timbers of his parents' home. Little remained.

It often rains in the mountains, and at certain times of the year a shower comes nearly every day. Obviously, it had rained several times on this burned out structure, erasing any clues that might have existed after the fire.

His mother had been so proud of this ranch, always keeping the yard cleared of weeds and clutter; she had even raised flowers along the front of the house. But now the weeds had grown tall all about, and suddenly the place looked as though it had been deserted for some time. The sight saddened Caleb.

Finally he returned to stand beside

the old prospector. From where he now stood, he could barely see the piles of rock that served as the final resting place for his parents. But he could not bring himself to go to their graves . . . that would have to wait for another time.

He studied the layout of the buildings. The ranch had been built on this long, narrow bench at the base of a sheer wall of limestone. The bench ran nearly four-hundred feet to his left and fell off very sharply to the grassy floor of the valley below. Off to his right, it lay some three-hundred feet then quickly rose fifty feet, continuing on for nearly an eighth of a mile. At the edge of that rise, only a few feet from the rock wall, the graves had been dug.

His dad had intentionally picked this site, which faced southwest toward Cochetopa Dome, to build upon, for its strategic location. The only approach was from the south, the western end of the bench being all but impossible to climb on horseback, the north and east being naturally guarded by the two-hundred feet high rock wall. A natural fortress, easily defended against any enemy. Yet their home had burned and they had died here.

'Let's ride, Grady.'

Having been unable to answer any of his questions, the two men returned to the barn and saddled their mounts. They were descending the narrow trail from the bench, when something caught Caleb's attention, something unconnected to the surrounding landscape.

Leaving the trail that angled from the bench down to the valley floor, he reined the paint to his left, dropping down the steep grade, sometimes sliding, to a small cluster of junipers some thirty feet below. There he reined in.

Stepping down from the leather, he walked the few remaining feet to a gnarled old conifer, then stooped, coming up with what appeared to Grady to be a club. Stepping back into the saddle, Caleb returned to the trail and held out the object.

Angrily he said, 'This answers a lot of questions, Grady.'

'What the . . . Lordy be! A torch! Weren't no accident a'tall, son. Them folks was murdered.'

Caleb was nodding. 'Looks like it, but I ain't surprised, since somebody's been tryin' to send me to perdition for nearly two months now. Let's get to town. They're gonna pay hob for this and its time to start rootin' out the culprits.'

Caleb had been desperate for answers. Now he had at least one. Murdered, yet he was not surprised. Crossing West Pass Creek, they rode down the valley toward Cochetopa Dome in silence.

It still remained for him to discover the identity of those responsible for the burning of the ranch houses and his parents' deaths. Also remaining to be discovered was the 'why' of it all. Suddenly, a thought burst into Caleb's mind and he reined in, turning in his saddle to face his companion.

'Grady, I've got to get to town and ask some questions, then I'll come back out here and have a better look around; I mighta missed a small clue. But I think the answer to why somebody's wantin' this place, lies up in those mountains where Dad was lookin' around.'

'Makes sense, Caleb, but like I done told ya, there ain't enough gold 'round yonder to pay a man fer his trouble.'

'I know that's what ya said, but Dad is . . . was a geologist. He knew rock formations and worked for a minin' outfit back fifteen years or so ago. I just can't believe he'd be traipsin' around up there without good reason.

'And Mom . . . she wouldn'ta gone with him, if he hadn't found somethin' worth messin' with. She'd studied geology and archeology, too, and was on those digs with Dad when they traveled over to Persia and Egypt. If she was with him, they had somethin' cornered up there. I'd bet my last dime on it.'

Grady gave thought to what Caleb said. He had known Angus and Abigail McConnell since shortly after they had moved into the area, and what Caleb said about the man devoting his time to a ghost trail made sense. His mother being an educated woman and having knowledge of rocks and rock formations made sense as well.

'Yeah, I'll go have a good look fer ya. I ain't shore what I'm lookin' fer, but I'll take me a ride up thataway.'

'Good, and thanks, Grady. Concentrate on the area where ya saw them camped, around Mount Ouray. If he spent time there, whatever he found oughta be in that neighborhood.'

So they parted company. Grady turned back to the north, toward Razor Peak Dome; Caleb continued south along the same route they'd traveled coming north.

He continued to ponder over the unanswered questions, but took time to enjoy his surroundings. Although the season was late for wildflowers, they were still plentiful. Looking down the valley, the green of the grass was the canvas upon which The Artist had brushed their beautiful array of colors, the entire painting being framed by the darker green of the pines mingled with the white, spotted bark of the aspen and their brightly colored leaves, some of which had already begun their metamorphous to yellow, gold, and orange. But he knew all too well that the beautiful portrait was soon to change.

Still, the sun was hidden by clouds, the peaks of the surrounding mountains blotted out by the foggy gray mist. Up there, the peaks would be receiving, at least, a dusting of snow; these valleys would soon join their ranks.

An hour before sundown, with the temperature dropping sharply, the cold wind picked up and snow began to fall. Had it not been for the blanket poncho he wore under his slicker, Caleb might well have been in trouble. As it was, he still shivered from the chill.

With the limbs of the trees and the scattered clumps of sagebrush already covered with the white crystals, Caleb emerged from the La Garitas and rode south of Twin Mountains. Three hours after sunset, a mile north of Del Norte, he entered a small stream that emptied into the river across from the town and followed it downstream.

At the mouth of the stream he quickly scanned the far bank, as best he could, then crossed the North Channel of the Rio Grande and urged the paint to climb from the icy water. Quickly he crossed the island, then forded the south channel of the river. At last, they stood once more on dry ground, at the end of Spruce Street.

He rode along the edge of town on Spruce Street, walking its length past Front and First Streets, then turned right, again walking the paint behind the buildings, finally pulling up outside the barn behind the Big River Hotel.

After seeing to his horse, Caleb slung

his saddle-bags over his right shoulder and, with his Winchester in his right hand, exited the barn and walked up the alley to the boardwalk that ran the length of First Street. There he stopped to have a look around.

Few people were about, for the temperature was now in the low teens, with at least three inches of snow on the ground. He was certain there was more to come.

Finally, he turned to the entrance of the hotel, the cold icy wind biting at his glowing red cheeks, and walked the few steps to the door, quickly stepping inside.

The sudden burst of heat, as he stepped through the door, was a welcomed one. A large iron stove in the corner glowed red, radiating wonderful waves of warmth, taking the first step to rid any weary traveler of the bone-chilling cold. He was glad to finally be inside, suddenly realizing he had forgotten just how quickly the weather could change at this elevation.

He had spent a few nights here, and always when he had been accompanied by Angel. Now he stepped to the desk and rang the bell. While he waited for the clerk, he signed the register. Finally the clerk appeared from the back and looked at the signature on his book. Immediately, his eyes widened and his breath caught. Suddenly Caleb was staring into the eyes of a very surprised and frightened man.

'We heard you were dead, Mr McConnell. The word's around town that you died down on the Staked Plain.'

'Word travels mighty fast . . . but those boys didn't quite get the job done. Oh, they thought they had, got three holes in me to prove it, but I'm here and they're feedin' worms down in Fort Sumner. Now, may I have my key?'

'Oh! I'm sorry, of course, Mr McConnell.'

So, with a trembling hand, the clerk handed him the key and Caleb marched wearily up the stairs and opened the door. It was a comfortable room, although very cold; he could see his breath with each exhale. The bed set along the wall on his left, a table holding a wash basin and pitcher sat between it and the window that looked out over First Street, and a coat tree stood in the corner to his right. Right of the window, in the corner across the room from the table, stood a small pot-bellied stove, with kindling and a pile of wood stacked in the middle of the wall on his right.

Dropping his rifle on to the bed next to his saddle-bags, Caleb opened the door of the stove and quickly put a fire together. Once the flames from the kindling spread to the larger sticks, he added more fuel, closed the door and adjusted the damper. Then he stepped back out into the hallway and proceeded down the stairs to have his supper.

The entrance to the dining room was across the lobby from the foot of the staircase, and as he strolled past the desk, the clerk watched him inquisitively. Caleb suddenly thought he must look pretty good for a dead man, and chuckled at the notion.

After having a quiet supper of beef and beans, he once again mounted the stairs and unlocked the door. When he again opened the door to his room, it was much more pleasant inside. He again added fuel to the fire and readjusted the damper.

He unloaded the Winchester and both converted Navy Colts, laying them out on the bed, then wiped them down, making certain each weapon was free of any moisture. Then he reloaded all three with fresh cartridges from a spare box kept in his saddle-bags. Suddenly he was dog tired.

Finally, he banked the fire for the night, then stretched out on the bed, again attempting to sort out what few clues he had obtained.

They amounted to little. But one thing was certain, two attempts had been made on his life and the houses on the Rafter MC had been intentionally burned, set afire with a torch, or torches. And his parents and the Urbanias were dead . . . *MURDERED*.

9

The stores along First Street were already opening as Caleb ate his breakfast. When he had finished eating, he stepped outside on to the boardwalk, retrieved the makings from his shirt pocket and rolled a smoke.

The sky had cleared and the sun shone brightly, reflecting off the snow, causing his eyes to water, making it difficult for him to see. Finally, he produced a match, slid it along the wall near him and put fire to his cigarette.

As he observed the few people who walked along the street, he saw a man step into Russell Conrad's mercantile. Before finishing his cigarette, he turned and walked in that direction. Coming to the door of the store, he flipped the butt into the snow-covered street, then turned the knob and stepped inside.

'Caleb? Is that you, Caleb?'

Caleb smiled at Russell Conrad, who had always been very nice to him. Even when he had been as old as fifteen years of age, the merchant had continued to give him candy from the jars on the counter, joking and laughing with Angus McConnell when he protested the gift.

'Yes sir, Mr Conrad. It's good to see you. How have you been?'

'Fine. Fine, we're all well, Caleb. Have you come home to stay, or are you just passing through? Caleb, we were all very sorry to hear about your folks. Angus and Abigail were two of the finest people I've ever known. I miss their visits.'

'Thank you, Mr Conrad. It was quite a shock. I only found out about it a couple of nights ago. And I ain't made up my mind yet, whether I'm stayin' or not.'

'Well, son, if you need *anything*, you come to me.'

'Thanks, Mr Conrad. I do need to purchase some warm clothes and a cold weather coat. I'm afraid my long johns are worn out, and this poncho just ain't gonna do the job.'

But before helping Caleb find the things he needed, Conrad motioned to a man of medium build with sandy hair, who stood near a shelf that held canned goods. He did not look like most of the 'city' men Caleb had met, who had fair skin and dressed like dudes. His skin was tanned and he dressed more like a Western man than an Easterner. He wore a gray Stetson, a black broad-cloth coat and flat-heeled riding boots with round toes.

'Caleb, I'd like you to meet our new school master, Mr Allen Snowden. Mr Snowden was hired last December, when Mr Lawson suddenly passed away. Mr Snowden, this is Caleb McConnell. His folks owned the Rafter MC. I suppose since they're no longer with us that makes Caleb here the owner.'

'How do you do, Mr McConnell,' the school teacher greeted. 'The entire town was certainly sorry to hear about your parents' tragic deaths. My sympathies, sir.'

'Thank you, Mr Snowden. Pleased to make your acquaintance.'

Snowden cordially made his departure, then Conrad came from behind the counter and sorted through the stacks of clothing on the tables, finding a heavy pair of corduroy breeches and a new pair of jeans, a new wool union suit, two heavy wool shirts and two pairs of wool socks. Finally stepping into the back, he brought out a new sheepskin coat and a pair of elk skin gloves, and had Caleb try on the coat for size.

'Well, son, that should 'bout do it. Those things oughta keep you nice and warm.'

Caleb added two boxes of .44s to the order as he pulled a gold eagle from his pocket. He was paying for the items, when Eva Conrad, the merchant's wife, entered the store, immediately followed by Lillian, their 19-year-old daughter.

When Lillian saw Caleb, her sparkling green eyes widened with her broadening smile.

'Mother, look who's come home,' Conrad joyfully announced.

Before Mrs Conrad could say a word, Lillian burst forward, swinging her arms around Caleb's neck.

'Caleb! Oh Caleb! It's so good to see you. I've missed you so.'

Embarrassed by the surprising show of affection, Caleb's face turned bright red and he was suddenly speechless. Besides that, he was being bombarded with questions that came so quickly, he had no hope of answering one before the next was being asked.

He and Lillian Conrad had been friends since his parents had moved into the neighborhood. They met during his first visit to the mercantile, when his family had stopped that first time to buy provisions, before continuing on to the ranch.

Back then, she had been a scrawny kid, only a couple of months younger than he, with stringy auburn hair, those beautifully large, round green eyes and freckles across her cheeks and nose. But now, had he seen her on the street, he doubted he would have recognized her.

She was five feet five inches tall and round in all the right places, although she still carried a shock of lovely auburn hair and a few freckles on her tiny, pert nose. Those large, green eyes were soft and warm, even though Lillian was so excited, and looking into them caused Caleb to melt, just a bit, inside. The ugly duckling he had known had turned into a majestic swan, for Lillian had grown into a beautiful, desirable, young woman.

While Lillian questioned Caleb, Conrad wrapped his purchases with brown paper and tied the bundle with string, making it easily carried with one hand.

Truly, he was happy to see Lillian, Lilly, as he knew her, but on this day he was in a mood, angry, depressed, suddenly lonely for his parents. He felt *all* of these things, but anger was the dominant emotion at present, and he wanted to be out of there, away from people so he could think.

A feeling was quickly building within him, the same feeling he had had while trailing Zaragoza's stolen herd of cattle, back down in New Mexico and West Texas.

'Well, Lilly, Mrs Conrad, if you ladies will excuse me, I'm sorry to have to rush off, but I've a few more errands to run. Mr Conrad, thank you. I'll be back for provisions, before I head back up to the ranch.'

Mrs Conrad stopped him before he could open the door. 'Caleb, of course you'll come for supper tonight, and I won't take 'no' for an answer.'

He wasn't certain he would feel like being around people, especially old friends. He doubted he would be very good company, but he had to eat.

'Of course, I'll come.' Then he looked again at Lilly and added, 'Might help me get outta this mood I'm in. Thank you, ma'am. Lilly, maybe I can answer all your questions tonight. Ladies,' and he tipped his sombrero.

He left the store and returned to his room. There he took the small coffee pot from his saddle-bags and filled it with water from the pitcher, placing it on the stove to heat. Then he banked his fire.

When the water was hot, he stripped to the skin, poured some of the water into the basin and bathed. After drying himself on the towel that lay next to the basin, he dressed in his new clothes, electing to wear the jeans instead of the corduroys, due to the noise they make when one walks. Dressed in his new duds, he stretched out on the bed to think. The room was pleasantly warm.

The pieces to the puzzle were still there. Where could he go and who could he ask to find the answers? Only a couple of names came to mind. But in spite of his mind working over the questions, the warmth from the fire penetrated his tired, tense muscles. Slowly, he relaxed and soon fell asleep.

10

The sun was at its zenith, when Caleb again stepped through the hotel door and on to the boardwalk. The temperature was much warmer now, perhaps in the forties, the sky was free of clouds and suddenly he felt good . . . *glad to be back at home*. That realization surprised him.

He rolled another smoke and put fire to it, then turned and walked down the alley, next to the hotel, and into the barn in the rear. He crushed his cigarette into the snow with his boot heel, before entering the barn.

Five horses stood in separate stalls, his own in the last stall on his left. He fed the paint a heaping measure of sweet feed and forked down some hay from the loft, then retrieved a brush from a shelf and ran it over the horse, brushing out the kinks in his long, black mane and tail. He finished his brushing and led the horse to the trough, broke the thin layer of ice with the axe that leaned near the pump, and let the animal drink his fill. He was once again tying the paint in his stall, when he heard voices.

Two men were carrying on a serious conversation as they approached the barn. Suddenly, a word caught Caleb's ear and he strained to hear more as they spoke.

'Simon ain't gonna like The Kid bein' 'round,' one man stated. 'Said that last note he got from the boss read mighty mean.'

'Won't make no difference, 'fore long,' the other responded. 'One of us'll run across him d'rectly an' that'll be the end of it.'

They stopped short of the door to finish their smokes, before entering the barn. Caleb remained quiet and unde-tected, listening to the continued conversation as he poked his new gloves behind the buckle of this gunbelt. Then he slipped the thongs from the hammer of both Colts.

'I ain't shore any one of us can take that kid,' the first man insisted. 'Him an' them other two played hob with our bunch over Zaragoza's cows that time, then he done fer Toby and Jake, later on in Eagle Pass . . . an' Toby Meacham were a shore 'nough daisy.

'And Rowdy told Lee that the old man, who seen that shootin' down at Sumner, said he'd never saw nobody move as fast as The Kid. Ole man said he seen Harden pull oncest, down to Texarkana, an' The Kid were faster'n him . . . g'arnteed it, he did.'

'That's a lotta *bull*, Red,' the second man scoffed. 'Ain't nobody faster'n John Wesley. But I shore hope we get this deal up here done in a hurry. I hate this dang cold weather. It gits cold, down in Texas, but I ain't never saw snow on the ground this early in the dang year. Reckon I wouldn't mind havin' me another big ole bonfire, to warm up my chilled bones, like the one we had up yonder at them cabins.'

With that being said, they put out their butts and walked through the door of the barn, stopping just inside to allow their eyes time to adjust to the lesser light.

Caleb, although peeking through the slats separating the stalls, was still concealed by the post at the end. Earlier, he had simply been in a surly mood, but after hearing what he had just heard, that old feeling of bloodlust overwhelmed him. He softly, coolly made his presence known.

'Howdy, Johnny,' he greeted pleasantly. 'Like I told Dieter and the Bauer boys, you fellas are a far piece off your range.' Then he stepped nonchalantly out into the open driveway, feet apart, hands near the walnut grips of his pistols.

To say the least, they were astonished to see him standing there — literally shocked. Suddenly faced by the man he had just proclaimed would be killed by any one of their outfit, Johnny Cathcart, a tall, lean, handsome young man, froze, unable to move a finger. Red Gibson, his lanky, long-haired companion, was no different. Suddenly faced to face with this trim package of certain death, Red wanted to be anywhere but where he now stood . . . but he could not move his feet.

'So y'all want another bonfire like the one ya had when ya burned my folks out, huh Red?'

'Look, Kid,' Red stammered, 'I didn't say that. Johnny — '

'Shut up, Red,' Johnny ordered.

'One of ya tell me about that fire,' Caleb demanded. 'I wanta know who was there and who sent ya to burn the place. I wanta know if my parents were shot, or if they died in the fire, and likewise for the Urbanias.'

Neither man spoke. 'One of ya better talk up and fast! My patience is wore plumb thin . . . and I'm just itchin' to kill somebody.'

'Kid, you better light a shuck for parts unknown. They's a price on yore head. A thousan' dollars, gold.'

'A thousand dollars, huh? You reckon to collect that bounty, Johnny? Well, I wouldn't go spendin' it quite yet. You ain't gotta ghost of a chance to collect it . . . not even with help.

'Red, you look like the smart one in this group. Why don't ya answer my question for me? Tell me what I wanta know, and I'll let ya ride outta here. *Who was there, Red?*'

Red Gibson swallowed hard. Suddenly there was a lump in his throat the size of a grapefruit. 'Kid, I . . . I ain't shore I oughta. Simon would skin me alive, Kid.'

Caleb had already heard the name, when they talked outside the barn. 'So Simon LaCrosse is here. And since you're here, Johnny, that means Lee is here, too. Since Dieter was one of 'em who tried to drygulch me down on the Llano, that would give cause to believe August is here with ya as well. Well, it's just like a homecomin' of sorts, ain't it, all you boys bein' here together. I reckon I'll be able to finish up that little fracas we had over them cows of Zaragoza's . . . as well as for my folks.

'Now I want an answer to my questions! Talk up, Red!'

Out of the corner of his eye, Red glanced at Johnny, who was standing rigid, staring into Caleb's cold, glaring eyes. Red was scared, that he would readily admit, but he was afraid to talk. He was relatively certain he was only seconds away from dying, here in this old, cold barn, but it would be a quick death, of that he was equally certain. However, if he talked, Simon LaCrosse would be just as certain to kill him, but most assuredly in an agonizingly slow, much more painful manner.

LaCrosse was a cold-blooded, vindictive, evil man, given to the sadistic enjoyment of watching his victims die slowly, painfully. Red had watched the man's eyes gleam with delight at the firing of the cabins on the Rafter MC, and with the agonizing screams coming from one of those same cabins.

'I ain't waitin' any longer, Red. Talk

up and ease your conscience, or die with it and explain it to the Judge.' Caleb flexed his fingers to keep them warm, and Red knew he was about to meet his Maker.

'Kid,' Red spoke quickly, 'Simon'll prob'ly kill me fer this, but we's all there, and nobody shot nobody that night.'

Caleb suddenly knew he would kill both of these men. He could taste the lust for blood, as if he were tasting coffee from a cup. He was mad clear through, but he still needed answers, so he held back the growing desire to kill.

'What about my parents, Red? So they died in that fire?'

Again Red swallowed, past the almost strangling lump in his throat. 'Kid, your folks — ' Red was cut short, for as he was speaking, Johnny Cathcart reached for iron.

With his gun barely out of its leather, Johnny was caught, just above the top button on his coat, by Caleb's first slug. Instinctively, Red's Remington was in his hand, but as its muzzle was about to level on his target, a .44 slug from Caleb's right-hand gun took him just above the belt buckle, and his shot went awry. When the second round struck him just below and right of his brisket, he came up on his heels, then toppled backward and lay gasping for breath, staring at the weathered rafters of the barn.

Caleb, now with both guns blazing, was still pouring lead into Johnny, who had not gone down with that first bullet, but had continued to fight, bringing his Schofield to bear. A bullet from Johnny's weapon burned Caleb's neck and struck a wood plank in the wall behind The Kid as he fired his third shot into the younger of the Cathcart brothers. Finally, with three slugs neatly grouped around that, now missing, top button, Johnny's Smith & Wesson .44 slipped from his unfeeling fingers and dropped to the straw-covered driveway. He sunk to his knees, then fell face down beside his weapon.

Caleb quickly bent forward, picking up a handful of dirt and straw, packing it into the fresh wound on his neck as he walked to Red's side.

Red still lay where he had fallen, frothy, pinkish blood coming from the corner of his mouth. Caleb stood over him, looking into his glazed eyes.

'Red, who's behind all of this. It's got to be somebody other than LaCrosse. *Give me a name, Red.*'

Red blinked his dying eyes. He heard the words Caleb spoke, and attempted to answer, but he could make no sound come from his lips. He could only cough, then his pupils widened and he relaxed, dead.

Caleb could hear the murmur of people gathering on First Street. Quickly he went through the dead men's pockets, finding only a folded slip of paper, some coins and a few odds and ends in Johnny's coat pocket. As he slipped the items into his own jacket pocket, he ran to the back door of the hotel, turned the knob and prayed it was not locked. It opened freely under his hand.

Quickly, he stepped inside the stockroom, where supplies for the restaurant were kept, and quietly closed the door behind him. Immediately, he brought his hand to the blood-clotted dirt on his neck, feeling for any blood that might have gotten on his collar. He rapidly slid out of the coat and inspected it, but found no obvious sign of his having bled upon it. He was thankful for that.

Then he ran his hand over his shoulder and collar of the shirt in an effort to determine whether or not they were stained. There did not seem to be any blood there, but without a mirror, he could not be certain. It being a maroon-colored shirt, blood would be less noticeable on it anyway.

But the dirt and straw had already stopped the bleeding from the scratch on his neck, so he removed the concoction and placed it near the door; there was little sign of blood in it. Then he pulled the large, black bandanna from his back pocket and tied it tightly around his neck, over the wound. Having done all he could to conceal his having been in a fight, he eased the door open, just a crack, so he could see the front of the barn.

All of those who had come to see what had happened, were standing just inside the entrance of the barn. The crowd was large enough so that he could not see the bodies of Johnny and Red, and all eyes appeared to be focused on the dead men.

The door hinges had made no noise, when he had first opened it, so he silently swung it open, kicked the emergency poultice of dirt and straw out through the opening, then stepped outside and quickly ground it into the snow. After quietly pulling the door closed, he stealthfully slipped around the corner into the alley and returned to the boardwalk.

He quickly scanned the street for anyone who might see him, and found no one near by. Breathing a sigh of relief, he walked to the door of the hotel and entered, climbing the stairs to his room.

After adding fuel to his fire, he removed his coat and shirt. There was a small hand mirror in the drawer of the table, so he brought it out and had a look at the bullet wound on his neck. It was, as he had believed, only a scratch and had not bled all that much.

Giving his shirt and coat closer inspection, Caleb found a light smear along the inside edge of his shirt collar, and a couple of drops had splattered on to the coat. Drawing his knife from its sheath, he carefully trimmed the stained spots from the tufts of wool that lined the collar, making certain not to cut away more than was necessary. Inspecting his tailoring, he decided that, without knowing where to look, one could not tell the collar had been altered. He ignored the light, inconspicuous smear on the shirt.

Now the adrenaline from the fight was used up and he was suddenly weary. He sat on the side of the bed and breathed deeply, trying to rejuvenate his jaded body. Then he remembered the items he had taken from Johnny Cathcart's pocket.

Retrieving the slip of paper, he unfolded it. There, written in black and white, were groups of names of men, three names per group, and water-hole locations, waterholes up and down the Llano Estacado. One of those groups of men consisted of Dieter Metzger and the Bauer brothers.

He was suddenly too tired to concentrate, to consider the significance of his discovery. But, now, finally and for whatever it was worth, he had proof that someone had gone to great lengths to have him killed. But why? And who?

He did not believe Simon LaCrosse would be the brains of the pack of dogs that had been sicced on him, but simply a tool used by someone else. LaCrosse was a hired gun, the epitome of evil, living only to destroy, kill, and see others suffer. He only hired on to see his employer's enemies wiped out, relishing in their misery. He had never shown the want for a home or to build anything, and for this reason, Caleb doubted LaCrosse was the one after the Rafter MC.

But here were facts explaining that twenty-one men had been deployed to seven different water-holes across the probable region through which he would travel north from Mexico. Whoever had conceived their plan, had known a great deal about him and had guessed well his likely route home. The information was little, but at least it was something, and more than he had before the shooting.

He again stretched out on his bed.

11

The Conrad home was not so different from those of Del Norte's other residences, built of log and stone. That is, until one stepped through the front door.

Inside, the house appeared to more likely belong in a large town or city, somewhere east of the Missouri. The furnishings had all been freighted in from St. Louis and Kansas City. Unlike the furniture of most of the homes in town, which were mostly made of split pine frames, straw-padded and covered by buffalo, elk or cow hides, there was no leather-covered furniture in their house; the divan and chairs were covered by lovely patterned fabric. Lace curtains hung over every window, and crocheted doilies were found on every table. The dining table was covered by a fine linen tablecloth, adorned by fine china, crystal and polished silver eating utensils.

It had been so long since he had lived with his parents in their lovely little cottage, at the edge of St. Louis, where he had slept, eaten and played. Like this home, that place had been immaculately kept by his mother, and he had felt warm and comfortable there.

Now, standing just inside the doorway of the Conrad home, Caleb was suddenly homesick, lonely. Even though he was freshly bathed and wearing his new clothes, he felt woefully out of place. The home of Ignacio Zaragoza was an extraordinarily beautiful hacienda, furnished with the roughly constructed furniture much like those of his parents' cabin, and he had always felt right at home there with Zaragoza.

But he felt a great kinship to the Conrads, a friendship much deeper than any other he had made after moving to Colorado, except for the closeness he had felt with Angel. Homesick and lonely he may be, but he was now glad to be here with friends.

Mr Conrad met him at the door, Lilly was close behind. After shaking Conrad's hand, Lilly took Caleb by the arm, escorting him to the comfortable, wine-colored divan, and seated herself next to him. Russell Conrad, seated in the heavy, brown arm-chair on Caleb's left, packed his pipe and lit it. As he exhaled, a large cloud of blue-gray smoke encircled his head.

'Well, Caleb, what have you been up to, these past three years?'

Caleb, who normally was quiet and reserved, was suddenly glad to talk. 'After I left here, I made my way down to South Texas and hooked up with an outfit down there. I trailed cattle up and down the country for a while, took ridin' jobs around Fort Davis and over along the west slope of the Eagle Mountains, then finally ended up down in Old Mexico, at a ranch along the Sabinas River.

'Most folks would say one ridin' job's like any other, but Señor Zaragoza is a good man and a real pleasure to work for, and he pays his hands well. I reckon he likes me well enough, because after a year or so, he made me segundo of the outfit. I's workin' for him, when I got the letter from Mom.'

Conrad again expressed his sympathies at the deaths of his parents and the Urbanias.

'Mr Conrad, what can ya tell me about Mom and Dad . . . over the last couple of years, I mean?'

Conrad seemed reluctant, pausing before answering, and Caleb wondered about the reason behind the hesitation.

'Caleb, you left because your dad sold his cattle and brought in a flock of sheep.'

'Yes, sir, that's true.'

'Well, he was very saddened when you left, maybe even heartbroken. But he and I talked about the move into the sheep business, a short time after you and Angel rode away.

'Your father was a highly educated man, who would never make a decision like that, without giving it a considerable amount of thought. The market for beef had continually fallen off and cowhides were practically worthless. So, he looked into diversifying. He considered the amount of land he had for pasture and how many head that graze would support, the market prices for the meat and for the wool. After doing some math, he thought it a better living than continuing on with cattle, so he bought the sheep.

'He told me once, he never made a major decision without first having your mother's input, so he talked about it with her, and after explaining all of the pros and cons, she agreed it was the wise thing to do.'

This revelation made Caleb feel small, self-centered and childish. He had so loved working alongside Angel, he had not considered what had led up to the decision to sell their cattle and bring in the sheep. How could he have been so foolish? Now, he could only sit and sadly stare into the fire.

'I reckon I was immature and impulsive, Mr Conrad. Angel was my best friend and mentor, so when he refused to work the sheep, I just followed suit. Well, I reckon we have to live with the mistakes we make, huh.'

'Well, Caleb, we live, we learn, and we move ahead. No sense looking back and stewing over it; it's water under the bridge.'

'I reckon you're right. But he'd already started wanderin' around up in the mountains, before I left, and I've been told he was stayin' away from the ranch more and more. Finally there, he got to takin' Mom with him. Can ya tell me *anything* about that?'

Again, Conrad hesitated, and Caleb was puzzled about that. Then, the man's eyes brightened, as if he had conquered some inner fear.

'I think I can, Caleb. Shortly before you left, he had been scouting for more grazing land, looking for any valleys or high country meadows, where he could pasture his stock. But you already know that.'

Caleb shook his head. 'I had no idea what he was thinkin' . Of course, I knew he was gone a lot, but he never bothered to let me in on what he was doin' . Dang it! If he'd only told me what was goin' on, I might notta pulled out, like I did. Dang it all!'

Conrad peered sympathetically at the young man next to his daughter, who sat quietly holding Caleb's hand.

'Well, he spoke to me about that, sometime later, Caleb. He truly regretted not having taken you into his confidence. But you were sixteen at the time, and, although you were doing a man's work, he simply didn't consider you mature enough to ask your opinion. I'm afraid it's a short-coming many fathers have, son, not talking to their children during times of crisis or when a decision is to be made, even though that decision will effect the entire family. But I *can* tell you, *without doubt*, he regretted not talking to you about it. He regretted it very much.'

Caleb could say nothing, only shake his head. He withdrew the makings from his shirt pocket, rolled a smoke, then lit it. But what had his father found in the mountains? Surely, it was something more than grass, for he had continued to go there, to the same area.

'OK, I can understand lookin' for more grass; a fella is always lookin' for pasture land. But it can't take forever to look those mountains over, and he kept goin' back to the same vicinity, over and over again. I've been told they were seen camped in the same spot on more than one occasion, and once for at least a week.'

Conrad considered this. 'Caleb, as you know, your dad and I were very good friends. But, he never came right out and told me what he expected to find up there. When he first told me that he was 'exploring', as he called it, I took for granted he was looking for gold. You know, we're not so far west of Pike's Peak, so, I figured he was simply prospecting.

113

'Then one day, back something like two and a half years ago, he came into town with some ore, the likes of which I'd never seen before. He had me box it up for him and arrange to send it all the way to Kansas City, to an assayer's office. Then eight, maybe ten, weeks later, he got an answer from Kansas City. I tell you, Caleb, he was so excited, I thought he was gonna bust his buttons.

'About a year later, he came in with another sample. We sent it off, but never got a reply from the assayer. That's when your mother started going off with him.

'Caleb, he never said as much, but I think he began taking her with him, because he was afraid for her. Don't ask me why, but I just got that feeling from him. I think he was afraid to leave her alone and unprotected, there at the ranch.'

Assay samples. Of what? Gold ore? Why was he afraid to leave his mother at the ranch? Caleb was pondering over this information, when Eva Conrad called them to the table.

They ate a delicious supper, and the talk around the table was light and pleasant. Conrad's business was good. Del Norte was a growing community and their future looked bright.

Lilly had only recently returned to Del Norte, however. For the past two years, she had lived with a family in Denver, and had gone to school there. It had been her long-time ambition to teach.

Now, even though the local school had an instructor, she hoped one day to teach there. After all, Allen Snowden, the current teacher, would certainly not stay there forever.

He was a relatively young, highly educated man, schooled in Europe, being fluent in five languages, and having excellent math skills. He knew literature, music, and geology, and had an in depth knowledge of ancient history and archeology. He had taken on the task of teaching there, only the year before, but, considering his age and extensive education, Lilly did not believe him the type of man to live out his life in a small town like Del Norte.

When the dishes had been washed, Mr and Mrs Conrad excused themselves and went to bed. Lilly and Caleb returned to the parlor, where she again seated herself next to him on the divan.

Their talk was light and pleasant, Lilly telling Caleb about her time in Denver and of her schooling. Then after a while, she got much more personal.

'I've missed you, Caleb, a great deal in fact. After you left, I just moped around for ever so long.'

'Over me leavin'? Why? We were always friends, but — '

'Caleb McConnell! You know very well, why. I've been in love with you since that first day your family came to town. I told you, once. *Oh, I can't believe you don't remember.*'

Suddenly Caleb did remember. He had not been interested in girls, back then, and she had been a scrawny freckle-faced nuisance, as far as he was concerned. But he did remember.

They had been young, and his interests lay with horses, cattle, and the work to be done around the ranch with his good friend, Angel. He had had no time for girls. But now, he was older, more mature and certainly interested in the ladies . . . and here she sat, a beautiful young woman.

'I'm sorry, Lilly,' he sputtered. 'But I do remember. My folks and I had come to town to get supplies. You and I were down at the livery, waterin' the horses, and you kissed me on the cheek and told me ya loved me . . . We were fifteen at the time. I remember, Lilly.

'But I was such a kid, back then. I reckon I musta been dumb as a post. Forgive me for that, will ya, Lilly?'

She held his hand and looked into his dark hazel eyes. She still loved him, after all this time, and she knew nothing would ever change that. What there was in him that had drawn her to him since their childhood, she could not say

117

exactly, but, what ever it was, it was still there.

For nearly two hours they talked. She expressed to him her desire for him to remain in the neighborhood, so she could see him often. How she knew it, she could not have said, but suddenly she knew he would stay; Caleb knew it, also. He would stay on the ranch, rebuilding the house on the bench near Cochetopa Dome.

Just as suddenly as she knew he would stay, she knew she no longer wished to be a school teacher. They would marry and she would work along side him on the ranch, keeping his house and bearing his children. In not too many years from now, a new generation of young McConnells would be riding alongside their father on the Rafter MC, and she would be there when they came home in the evening. *But then she could still be a teacher*, for she would have the privilege of schooling her own children.

12

Leaving Lilly, Caleb cautiously walked along the west edge of town toward the river, then down the full length of Front Street, warily keeping to the shadows, suspicious of any place where danger might await him. Finally, he approached Aaron Johnson's livery.

He opened the narrow side door and stepped through, stopping inside at the entrance to Aaron's quarters. Light from inside the room showed through the cracks in the wall and around the door, so Caleb softly knocked.

Aaron Johnson was a tall, lanky, stooped-shouldered man in his early fifties. He had few teeth, none in the front, and Caleb had never seen the man when he did not have a huge chew of tobacco in his jaw. Even though the hour was late, this night would be no different, for the great chew was there, making Johnson's right cheek bulge with its mass.

'Howdy, Caleb, heared you's back in town,' Johnson cheerfully greeted. 'I ain't seen you in a coon's age, boy. Danged if'n you ain't growed into right smart of a man.'

'Howdy, Mr Johnson. Yeah, I reckon I've sprouted some.'

'Mr Johnson, be durned, boy. Growed men call me Aaron, an' I reckon you're growed enough. What can I do fer ya, son?'

Caleb chuckled at the hostler. 'Alright, Aaron, and thanks. I'm needin' to rent a horse from ya, if ya have a good mount available. My paint's over in the barn back of the hotel, and he's a mighty good mount, but we've seen a lot of country, since leavin' Fort Sumner, and he's about played out. Have ya got somethin' I could use for a week or so?'

'Well, first off, you ain't gonna rent no horse off'n me, no sir. Why, you and yore folks has been good friends to me, over the years. Yore maw and paw was the salt-o-the-earth, an' I shorely hated it when I heared 'bout that fire what took 'em.

'But I got a big ole strawberry roan back yonder in the corral that were just re-shod day-b'fore-yesta-day, an' I'll loan 'im to ya fer as long as ya need. He's a mustang, mountain bred, but as loyal as a ole heel-hound. He takes on, oncest in a while, but I'd say you could ride 'im down in a short. He's shore-footed, got speed and plenty of bottom. He oughta make ya a good mount, and he's yore'n fer the askin' . Yore we'come to 'im.'

After thanking the old man for his generosity and explaining he would return for the roan after the town was asleep, Caleb, using caution to stay in the shadows, went back to his hotel, built up his fire, packed his belongings, then blew out the lamp and turned in for a couple of hours' sleep.

★ ★ ★

It was nearing 2.00 a.m. when Caleb pulled his sombrero down on his head, swung his gunbelt around his waist and tied his holsters down. When he had once again checked the loads in each of his weapons, he donned his sheepskin coat and quietly made his way down the stairs into the lobby, slipping undetected out through the front door of the hotel to the boardwalk outside. Quickly and silently, he dropped his war-bags in the barn behind the hotel and picked up his bridle, tucking it inside his coat to warm the bit.

Again, staying to the shadows, he walked to Johnson's livery. There he slid the warm bit into the roan's mouth, slipped the head stall over his ears and fastened the throatlatch. Now leading the roan, he traveled along the dark passages of a different route, returning to the barn behind the hotel.

Leaving the roan tied outside to a post, he cautiously slipped into the barn, a Colt in each hand, sliding to his left and into the darkness of the first stall, squatting there for what seemed like forever. Finally, being certain there was no one laying for him inside the barn, he walked back outside and led the horse in.

He quickly threw his saddle on the roan and cinched it tight. Then he slid the Winchester into the boot and tied his saddle-bags and bedroll behind the cantle.

Mounting the strawberry roan, Caleb turned left out of the barn, circling the building to its rear and putting it between himself and the town. He had no illusions about there not being someone watching for him, for he believed he had been under constant observation since his arriving from New Mexico. But if he had been able to slip from the hotel and leave town without their knowing about it, at least for a while, it would give him a head start for the country north of the Rafter MC.

As is common with late summer weather in the Rockies, the temperature had risen and most of the snow had already melted. However, the night was cold, and he was sorry he had not been able to sleep in his warm, cozy hotel room. But he was bound for the country north of Marshall Pass and the valley down which Starvation Creek flows. He was going to the place where Grady Bolton had seen his parents camped.

It had finally come to him that to get to the bottom of his parents' murders and of the attempts to kill him, he must first discover the reason behind it all. What was there in those mountains north of the Rafter MC that made the deaths of a half dozen people necessary? He hoped finding the reason would answer at least some of his questions, and give him a clue with which he could answer the rest.

Approximately three hundred yards south of the barn, Caleb rode the big roan down into a shallow wash that ran northeast, into the river, and followed along its sandy bottom. At the mouth of the wash, he coaxed the roan into the icy water and they crossed the south channel of the Rio Grande, coming out of the water in the aspen and cottonwood grove on the island that separated the two channels of the river.

Amidst a small grove of aspens, at the edge of the island, Caleb pulled up, listening for any sound of pursuit. But he heard only the gurgling sound of the churning water in the river, as it swiftly flowed over the rocks. He heard the rustling of the leaves overhead, but nothing more . . . not even the chirping of crickets.

Having heard no sound that was out of the ordinary, he moved the roan across the small island, hesitating on the northern bank, then giving the roan his head and crossing the north channel. Once on the other side, he stepped down, wrapped his hands around the knee of the horse and squeezed as he ran his hands down all four legs of the tall animal. When he had removed as much of the water as possible, he stepped back into the saddle.

This roan loved to travel, and for a while Caleb allowed him to move at his own pace, which was a quick one. The horse strode with long, smooth strides, eating up the ground quickly.

Riding north, Caleb eventually lifted him to a lope, keeping the horse moving through the foothills along the eastern slope of La Garitas. Avoiding any place where danger might await him, as the sun rose over the peaks of the Sangre de Cristos, he reined the roan to a halt and stepped down from the leather. There, both man and horse drank deeply from Carnero Creek.

Another hour in the saddle found Caleb turning north, up the north fork of Carnero Creek. Two miles up that fork, he found a shallow, open depression that was nearly encircled by large slabs of limestone, thrust upward through the earth's surface, lying bare and exposed to the elements. Pulling up in that depression, he again stepped out of the leather.

He was tired, and he had pushed the

horse hard, hoping to be far ahead of any pursuit. Both were in need of some rest, so he unsaddled and staked the roan on the lush grass inside the circle of rocks, built a small fire and made coffee. As the coffee boiled, he spread his bedroll on the ground among the boulders. When he had eaten some elk jerky and drank the coffee, he rolled into his blankets and slept.

After two hours, Caleb awoke, feeling refreshed, and both he and the roan were ready to move out. It had been several years since he had ridden this country, but he located the trails, of which he knew, with little difficulty.

Again he rode the game trails, traveling along the sides of the mountains and staying to the timber as he rode. At this altitude, there remained some snow, and twice he came upon washes where the snow had drifted four to five feet deep, forcing the roan to struggle to traverse them.

An hour before sundown, and riding a trail upon which he had never been,

Caleb came to the edge of a slide, reined in and stepped down.

Nearly one hundred yards across, the shale slide fell off steeply to his right for over a thousand feet. A man on foot should have little trouble crossing it, but a horse could be something else, and this was the first time he had ridden this animal and knew nothing of him. If the roan became nervous, balked, or shied, Caleb might well find himself afoot in these mountains, miles away from shelter and food.

He could go back the way he had come, but he liked nothing about that alternative. Somewhere behind him, he was certain, they were following, and if he had not hidden his trail well enough, they would be there to block his retreat.

'Well, Red, whatdaya think? I hope you're as good as Ole Aaron thinks ya are.'

Johnson had insisted this roan was a mountain-born mustang, surefooted and steady, so Caleb, trusting the horse to keep his head and cross the slide safely, led the way. Twice the roan slipped, sending a cascade of shale down the mountainside, the sound of the sliding, bounding rocks echoing down the canyon.

But the mustang remained calm, kept his feet under him and recovered quickly. Slowly, cautiously, they crossed the slide, and when they reached the far side, Caleb breathed a tremendous sigh of relief and patted the big mustang on the neck.

Back in the leather, they continued along the game trail, until it began to fade in the gathering darkness under the dense pines that covered the mountain. As the sun disappeared below the unclad, ragged, inhospitable peaks of the Cochetopa Range, Caleb again stepped down, this time a hundred yards off the trail in a small clearing, deep within a thick stand of low-hanging pines.

The night air at that altitude was cold, and Caleb's small fire did little to fight off the chill. But he dared not build a larger one, for although the dry pine made nearly no smoke when burned, the air cools with the setting of the sun and drifts down the mountainsides, carrying with it the aroma of the burning wood, down into the valleys and canyons below. Even his small fire was a risk, but the light and smoke given off by a large fire would be an open invitation for his enemies to join him.

He quickly ate a small supper and drank a pot of coffee. Then he buried a few of the coals from the fire, beneath a few inches of earth, and spread his ground sheet and blankets over them. Finally, he turned the collar of the sheepskin coat up to cover his ears, pulled the sombrero down tightly on his head, and rolled into his blankets.

The heat from the buried coals soon penetrated his body, and within minutes his muscles relaxed and he slept comfortably.

13

Mid-morning of the next day found Caleb riding north along the edge of what was known as 'Big Dry Gulch'. An hour before noon he turned west and rode up Rabbit Canyon.

He had intended to explore the area around the place where his parents had camped on Starvation Creek, but while riding in the clear, cool hours just after sunup, he remembered Grady Bolton might already be back at the ranch, awaiting his return. Grady might have some answers for him . . . at least that is what Caleb hoped.

Now the temperature was well into the sixties and what snow remained was melting quickly, making travel through the mountains, at least at the lower elevations, much easier. So, staying to the edge of the timber along the canyons and draws, before three in the afternoon, he crossed the divide through Cochetopa Pass and made his way down the canyon where West Pass Creek begins, finally sitting the roan below the bench where the remaining buildings of the Rafter MC stood. The sun was a fiery orange ball perched atop Sawtooth Mountain, when he saw the thin line of wood smoke rising from the bench. Grady was back.

'How is it, son?' Grady greeted, when Caleb stepped down near the fire and took his cup from his saddle-bag.

Without saying a word, Caleb handed the old prospector the slip of paper he had taken from the body of Johnny Cathcart. When the old man finally grasped the meaning of what was written there, he looked up at his young friend and nodded.

'They shorely had ya staked out, boy. Somethin' like this here takes plannin', and plannin' of this sort takes some mighty sharp thinkin'. You got any idy who in that outfit's got gumption enough to lay out somethin' like this?'

Before he could answer, Grady suddenly had a thought and asked, 'Where'd you git this?'

Caleb shook his head. 'Off the body of one of their outfit; we've got two less to deal with, when the time comes,' to which the old man grinned and nodded.

'Grady, I know all those boys in that bunch, and I reckon there's only one of 'em who might have the brains to come up with somethin' like this.

'But none of those ole boys are from around here. I don't reckon any of 'em knew where I was from, 'cause I never talk about myself or this country much, and only told folks I's from somewhere in Colorado. I made sure not to mention the Cochetopa country at all.

'Simon LaCrosse leads 'em, and he's a sorry excuse, if ever there was one. But there's nothin' up here he'd be interested in, unless it was on four hoofs or was already dug outta the ground. He's a thief and a hired gun. It don't appear they're lookin' to steal cattle, and I guarantee ya he ain't after those sheep, so I've got to think they've been hired by *somebody else* to rid the country of McConnells. And there still lies the question. *Why?*'

'Well,' Grady offered, 'I ain't shore what it is they's lookin' fer, but they's somethin' goin' on up yonder 'round Starvation Crik an' Mount Ouray.'

Grady had Caleb's attention. If they could uncover the reason why someone wanted the Rafter MC, he might be able to identify the man behind the plot.

'What'd ya find, Grady?'

'Well, son, I's headed up yonder to have me a look around, but when I come to where Quartz Crik empties into Tomichi Crik, I found a track.'

'So what's so strange about that?'

'Son, it were a mighty small track, a single track. Whoever made that track were doin' some fancy work to cover his trail. So right then I give up on Starvation Crik an' turned back down Tomichi, lookin' fer more sign of him

. . . an' I found 'em, an' more.

'A mile or so down stream, there were some grass broke over an' the edge of a heel print. Further along I foundt a toe print. Twicest I found a bit of another fella's track and oncest a scuff mark on a rock, made by a horseshoe. They's doin' a right fair job of coverin' their trail, but all them tracks I seen was headin' downstream.

'That give me a idy, so I ups an' light's out fer Gunnison. I stayed yonder fer two days, and visited all three saloons. I just listened, mostly, but inquired 'round if anybody'd saw any strangers about. Fin'lly one feller mentioned some folks ridin' in, leadin' a jackass.

'When I asked fer 'em at the general store, I's told the same thin' . A couple of prospectors come in fer their supplies, ever' couple of months or so. Storekeeper said it'd been more'n a month since they's in last. Said that were the fourth time, in the last year or so, them folks'd been yonder, getherin'

135

enough grub an' such to last 'em a couple of months or more, each time they visited him.

'That storekeeper ain't the brightest candle in the chandelier, son, and he ain't the kind to be too nosy, so he couldn't give me much of a description. B'sides, one of them fellas always stayed outside with the animals.

'They's already gone from Gunnison, when I got there . . . got their grub an' pulled out. Musta saw me trailin' 'em an' hid-out whilst I passed 'em by, but I'd betcha a nickel-to-a-donut they's back up yonder in them mountains right now.

'Caleb, them tracks might have nothin' to do with you a-tall, but they's somethin' queer 'bout this whole deal. I reckon I just ain't smart enough to sort the whole dang thin' out.'

Caleb was doing some sorting of his own. Grady smoked quietly and poured coffee from the pot into Caleb's cup. After several minutes of silence, Caleb rose and walked to the roan. He picked up the reins and led the horse to the barn and stripped the gear, then ran a brush over him, all the while mulling over this new information.

Two men were looking about the region where his parents had looked. The 'who's behind it all' question might be answered if he could find those men, and ask the right questions.

At last, Caleb returned to the fire, where the old man was placing thick elk steaks in a skillet. 'Grady, we'll spend the night here and head for Starvation Creek in the morning. If we find somebody up there prowlin' around where my folks were doin' their prospectin' , they'll explain why, or somebody'll take a beatin' . If they wanta make a fight of it, I can take care of that, too.'

14

When the sun painted its first streaks of pink across the wispy clouds overhead, it found Caleb and Grady riding north of Razor Creek Dome. Staying on the valley floor, they skirted the steep slopes until they rode into Tomichi Creek, at the mouth of the long canyon through which the creek flows.

With Grady on the north, Caleb on the south, the two men began their dissection of the banks of the creek. At the mouth of Quartz Creek, Grady showed Caleb where he had found the first heel print.

'Weather's wiped it out, son, but right here's where I seen it.'

'Keep lookin' , Grady. We gotta find somethin' that'll lead us to those fellas.' So they kept searching.

Approximately four miles up the creek the canyon split, forming two

138

separate canyons. Tomichi Creek turned sharply into the northern fork, and they followed it. Another mile found them at the mouth of Marshal Creek.

Tomichi Creek continued north toward its head-waters, but they now rode along Marshal Creek, which came from the east, and the Starvation Creek country. Still, they had found no sign of anyone traveling the neighborhood. But Caleb knew they were there — he could feel them.

Another two miles of searching revealed nothing, so at the mouth of Big Bend Creek, Caleb called Grady to join him on the south bank. Both men stepped down and Caleb put a fire together, Grady filled the pot and dumped a handful of coffee into it. Then, both men sat near their small fire and smoked, while they waited.

'Son, I know we've had some weather, since I seen them tracks, but a fella'd think he could find some little sign of them folks.'

'You'd think,' Caleb responded. 'They're

better at hidin' a trail than we gave 'em credit for.'

Back in the saddle, still covering both banks, they slowly made their way to the head of Marshal Creek. Another quarter of a mile up the mountain found them sitting in Marshal Pass. Caleb sat the roan and sighed heavily.

'Grady, I swear, I've got no idea what we're lookin' for or where to look for it.'

Grady chuckled. 'Well, son, I'll admit, it feels like we's lookin' fer a needle in the wrong haystack, but them fellas gotta be in this neighborhood. An' unless they's holed up some'heres, they're gonna make some tracks. I reckon I shoulda backtracked them two when I first seen them tracks, but I got all het-up an' fig'red I's doin' the right thin' by goin' to Gunnison.'

'Don't worry about it,' Caleb quickly responded. 'I mighta done the same thing, had I been in your moccasins. Let's drop on down a ways and pull up for the night. Poncho Creek's just b'low here and I know a good spot down yonder.'

So he urged the roan forward and within an hour they pulled up in a long, narrow, aspen covered depression, a few yards from the banks of Poncho Creek.

That night, beside their fire, they talked of the men they sought. Grady was convinced that, like himself, they had observed Angus McConnell during one of his excursions into the area, and had become convinced he had good reason to be prospecting there. Gold had been uncovered on all sides of these mountains, and it made sense to him there would be more to be found here. After all, he believed it was here and had spent a good many years searching in this same region.

But knowing his dad as he did, Caleb was not convinced. Certainly, Angus McConnell was a knowledgeable, experienced geologist, but he was not a man to go off half-cocked on a gold-hunting spree. Caleb recalled his dad's attitude about gold hunting and his opinion of gold hunters. He remembered the repugnant manner in which his dad had spoken on the subject.

'I don't know, Grady,' Caleb answered as he shook his head. 'Until somebody proves me wrong, I'll never b'lieve Dad caught the gold fever.

'If he was up here lookin' for range for those dang sheep, he'd have hunted up every valley, meadow and mesa in these mountains. With that in mind, I'm gonna do the same thing. We're gonna look for any place a fella could graze his stock. That's the only way I can think of for us to locate what he found. Maybe we can get lucky.'

They were relaxing, smoking and drinking their coffee, as the fire burned down to coals. Suddenly, Caleb had an idea.

'Grady, would you go back to Gunnison and send a message over the wires for me?'

Grady nodded.

'Sure, son, I'll do whatever ya need did.'

Caleb reached inside his saddle-bag and brought out a small tablet and the stub of a pencil, scribbled out his message, then took a gold eagle from the pocket on his chaps. When he handed them to Grady, the old man read the message, then looked up sharply.

'What's this about?'

'We don't know what Dad was lookin' for, but he sent samples to Kansas City to be assayed. They'll have a record of that assay report, and I wanta know what's in it. There might be somethin' in there that'll ring a bell with you, too. I don't know how else to do this.

'You wait for an answer to this telegram, while I look for that pasture land we're talkin' about . . . and buy more grub, while you're there. Unless you've got another suggestion.'

Grady first nodded, then shook his head, and Caleb laughed at his apparent uncertainty. 'What, Grady?'

'Well, fer the first time since we

started down this road, I reckon we're on the right track. They's a good bit of information in them reports, and ya might be right, 'bout there bein' somethin' in it what might strike a note fer me.

'But even if there weren't no color in that sample he sent, them other minerals named in that report just might help me fig're out where he were lookin'. I shoulda thought about doin' this b'fore now.'

For the first time in weeks, Caleb had the feeling things were looking up. Grady would wait for an answer from Kansas City, and, while the old man was gone, he would make good use of his time by scouring the countryside.

* * *

Caleb peered down through Marshall Pass, as Grady disappeared on the other side. He knew this country fairly well, having ridden it with Angel on several occasions.

Together, he and the *vaquero* had done as, he believed, his dad had done, searching the region for possible grazing land. While doing so, they had located a number of high country meadows that would support a sizable herd for most, if not all, of the summer.

Having decided to divide the surrounding country into four sections, Caleb turned the roan north and rode toward Mount Ouray. Less than an hour went by and they walked from the timber into a long meadow, where Caleb reined in.

Crossing his right leg over the roan's neck and wrapping it around the saddle-horn, Caleb relaxed, tipped back his sombrero and pushed a hand inside his coat, pulling the makings from his shirt pocket. He put paper and tobacco together, rolled it tightly, then ran his tongue along its length and sealed it. Finally, striking a match with his thumbnail, he put fire to it and drew deeply. While he smoked, he surveyed the meadow.

It swept over a rolling park, laying over a mile to the west, and was over a half mile wide. Steep jagged walls bordered the park on the north and south, and the tall grassy meadow was surrounded by a mix of aspen and pine. After only a few minutes, he was certain this was not the place where his dad had concentrated his attention, but at least he had found an excellent source of summertime grass.

★　★　★

For the next five days, Caleb scoured the country. During that time, he found more than a dozen meadows where he could graze stock, once he replenished his herd.

Beside his fire at night, he thought of his parents and of their deaths. Someone was going to pay for that . . . and they would pay with blood. He had no doubt LaCrosse had given the orders, but there was someone else behind the plot to obtain the Rafter

MC . . . there had to be.

He also thought of Lilly, of her beauty and of how he had thought so little of their friendship when he was younger. Only a few nights before, she had told him she had loved him for years, but he had never realized how she felt.

He had deserted his parents, and he had deserted her as well. It sorrowed him, now, how a young man can hurt those who love him by being so impetuous and inconsiderate. But he was back, and he would stay. But what of his reputation?

While riding for Ignacio Zaragoza, the Sabinas Kid had built quite a reputation, one that brought confidence to those who rode with him, and caution and doubt to those whom he rode against. But that was hundreds of miles south, and here in these starkly beautiful mountains of Colorado, the Sabinas Kid and his reputation would be forgotten quickly . . . so he hoped.

For those five nights, he slept soundly

and faced each day with new hope of finding what he sought. But each day brought more disappointment, for all he found was more pasture for his stock. Eventually, he became discouraged.

15

On the morning of the sixth day, Caleb rode back to the depression near Poncho Creek, where he and Grady had camped. Long before he reached the place, he knew Grady had already returned, for he was still nearly a half mile away, when he smelled the smoke from the old man's fire.

Caleb walked the roan into the camp and stepped down, loosened the cinch, then broke out his cup.

'Got that answer to yore wire, son,' Grady offered.

He handed the message to Caleb, then watched for a reaction. The message read:

Caleb McConnell:
Assay office broken into and ransacked. Several reports stolen, including report to Angus McConnell. Matter

turned over to office of US Deputy Marshal. He will contact you immediately.

However, I remember sample to be primarily kimberlite.

Isaac Samuels, Chief Assayer

Grady could see the puzzlement on Caleb's face.

'What the devil is *kimberlite*, Grady?'

The old prospector removed his hat and scratched his shaggy head. 'I ain't shore, son. Seems I heared it mentioned oncest upon a time, but I can't recollect what were said about it. But whatever it is, yore pappy musta set some store by it, fer he sent more'n one of them samples of the stuff to be assayed.'

Well, Caleb had gotten an answer, but he had no idea what that answer meant. He must find out more about this kimberlite.

'Let's finish our coffee and head back to Del Norte. Maybe somebody there can tell us what this *kimberlite* is.

'I've covered this whole dang country, except for the area north of where Starvation joins Poncho Creek. Why don't we circle that way and have a quick look-see? We can head out around the east face of Mount Ouray, then turn northwest and cross back over through Monarch Pass.'

When the coffee was gone and the fire extinguished, they tightened their cinches and stepped up. Caleb led the way down Poncho Creek, past the narrow canyon he had designated as the landmark to separate his two 'search areas' north of the creek.

When they drew close to the confluence of Poncho and Starvation Creeks, Grady pointed out the place where he had seen Angus and Abigail McConnell camped, on at least two occasions; a blackened ring of stones marked the spot. Just downstream from that campsite, Caleb found another game trail and turned the roan northwest on to it.

They traveled slowly, looking for any

sign of something being out of place or strange to the country, and for a track; only the fresh tracks of elk, big horned sheep, and mule deer showed on the trail. They found nothing, as the sun rose above them and the temperature warmed into the seventies, a steady breeze rustling the pine needles overhead.

Now the trail stretched out along the girth of the mountain, upon a narrow bench, and they rode high-up on the mountainside, at the upper edge of the trees only a few yards below timberline. They were circling a point, where the mountain extended a finger out away from its bulk, approximately one and a half miles north of Poncho Creek and only a few hundred yards south of Gray Creek, when the trail turned and circled the point, rising sharply along the stark face of the mountain above timberline.

From the trail, the mountain fell sharply away, but the two riders forced their animals down through the timber, diagonally, riding a switchback pattern to ease the climb down, Grady's mules managing the descent better than the roan.

After finally reaching the bottom, they crossed a narrow flat, and were ready to ford Gray Creek, when Grady abruptly reined the mule in.

'Caleb, looky here,' he said, as he pointed to the ground, near the edge of the creek, and stepped from the leather.

Caleb turned the roan to face the old prospector, then joined him on the ground. Grady waved his hand over a small patch of grass that had been bent over, showing the evidence of something passing. Then he spread the spindly stems of grass and nodded. There in the soft earth was a slight imprint, a small, narrow shape of a boot, and near it was the impression of the edge of a horse's hoof.

Caleb's breath quickened. Here before him was what they had searched high and low for, for more than a week. He ran the palm of his left hand over the butt of the Colt hanging at his hip. He would question the maker of this track, and the answers he received in return had better be good ones . . . and the right ones.

'Headed downstream, Caleb. Headed back to Gunnison, I'd reckon.'

'Well, we're gonna backtrack 'em and see what they've been up to. Let's amble.'

Stepping back up, Caleb slid the Winchester from its scabbard. They turned their mounts upstream along the timber-covered southern bank of Gray Creek, finding a track here, a bent blade of grass there. There was no bank on the north side of the creek, for the path of the swiftly flowing stream followed along the sheer wall of the mountain.

Once, they found the track of a larger man, not so deep as the track made by a heavy man, but a bootprint a bit larger than the first track they had found. Slowly, carefully they followed the creek upstream.

Only a few minutes later, they came to a narrow canyon, a mere crack in the face of the rock down through which the creek flowed. A passage only five feet wide, its walls hundreds of feet high, the place had an eerie feeling about it.

'Keep a weather eye, son. Ain't no tellin' what we're fixin' to walk into. I don't like the look of this place nary bit.'

'I gotcha, Grady. You keep an eye on our backtrail. I'd hate like the devil to get caught here in this narrow canyon, by somebody comin' up on us from behind.'

Caleb reined the roan into the stream and urged him into the narrow passage, the mustang walking through the opening without hesitation. For nearly a quarter of a mile, they walked in the water, Grady's mule right on the roan's heels. Suddenly, the mustang stepped out of the canyon into more timber.

Caleb looked to his right and left, finding the smooth, towering walls suddenly breaking away from him, the creek following along the wall on his right. Talus littered the base of both walls, a thick stand of mixed aspen and pine covering the landscape away from them.

He eased the roan forward, squeezing the small of the rifle stock, ever mindful of the danger into which he might be riding. He went only a short distance further and walked the roan out of the timber, into an open area that must have been nearly a mile long, a half mile wide, completely encircled by the sheer rock wall; they were in a box canyon.

The ground that lay before him appeared to be a large hump in the center of the canyon, with only a few branches of the treetops on the far side showing above it. Only a few feet outside the timber, the open ground rose slightly, sparse grass, only a few scraggly junipers and scattered sagebrush growing along its slope. He nudged the roan forward, moving up the shallow grade to the top. Once again, he reined in, Grady's mule stepping up beside him on his right.

Now they sat their mounts on the top of a deep bowl, a basin, the bottom of which was clearly deeper than the place where they had entered the valley. Along the inner slope, nothing grew; no grass, no junipers, nothing. In the bottom of that bowl, at its northern end, was a patch of bluish dirt, estimated by Caleb to be two hundred yards long, fifty or sixty yards wide. In the northwest corner of that patch, there were signs of a dig.

Unwilling to descend the inner slope, for fear of being trapped down there without cover and no way to get out without being exposed to gunfire from above, Caleb motioned Grady to move along the rim of the bowl, surveying its bleakly naked bottom as they rode.

When they reached its northern end, Caleb led the way back down the outer slope of the basin. At the edge of the timber, he reined in again, for a few feet from where he sat the roan, stood a small cabin. Nodding toward the tiny log building, Caleb rode forward, as Grady sided him, surveying the area for any sign of its occupants. But no one seemed to be at home.

The cabin was approximately fifteen feet wide and ten feet deep, constructed of notched pine logs, chinked with mud to seal the cracks between them. It was a place large enough for two men to live comfortably.

At the front door, both men stepped down and looked carefully around, still searching for the occupants, but admiring the work of those who had built it. Then Caleb lifted the latch and they stepped inside.

On their left stood a small table and two chairs, all three pieces made from materials that surrounded the cabin. A clean tin plate and cup sat on either end of the table. Immediately to their right, a large bed had been constructed, then covered with grass-filled bags and two elk skins, to make a mattress. Two large comforters were spread neatly over it. In the back, right corner of the cabin, stood a small, cast-iron, pot-bellied stove, a *caboose* stove, into the door of which was cast the words, Denver-Rio Grande Railroad. The place was immaculately well kept.

Caleb crossed the room and placed his hand on the top of the caboose stove. Cold. Then he and Grady searched the place for any clue that might help them know these men better.

In the back left corner was a blanket, folded neatly, lying on a section of tree trunk that served as a table. Somehow, to Caleb, the blanket looked out of place, so he walked over to it. When he raised the blanket, he found a small leather sack nearly filled with crystalline rocks, all partially covered with traces of the dried, bluish clay from the bottom of the basin.

Caleb examined them closely, then handed one to Grady. 'What are we lookin' at, Grady?'

The old prospector examined the

jagged, peasized stone carefully, then shrugged.

'Dogged if I know, son. I ain't never saw this blue clay b'fore, an these here quartz rocks look like . . . quartz rocks, to me.

'This here quartz could be the dredges left from workin' gold from a vein of the stuff. But they's no dolly pot here . . . an' the only way I knows how to separate gold from quartz is by grindin' the quartz up in the bottom of a dolly pot, then pickin' out the color. It's sorta like them Mexican women does, when they grind up their corn fer their tortillas, only a dolly pot's a sight bigger an' heavier'n them little stone bowls they uses. But if that ain't what we're a-lookin' at here, I got no idy what these fellas are up to.'

Caleb simply shook his head. The stones were nearly all the same size, small and of varying shapes from extremely rough and jagged to round and smooth. Only a few were as large as a man's thumbnail, and all of those were very rough. But why would someone bag up the quartz after separating it from the gold it held?

He returned the crystals to the bag, keeping one of the larger stones, one a bit smaller than a .32 slug, which he placed in the watch pocket of his jeans. Finally, he placed the bag back in the corner under the blanket. They found nothing else of interest inside the cabin.

Having seen all they could see, Grady walked outside and packed his short-stem pipe with tobacco from a large Cheyenne-made, beaded, leather pouch. By the time he held his lighted match over the bowl, Caleb was joining him near the roan.

'Well, what's next, son?'

Caleb thought carefully about what his next move should be. His father had sent his samples to Kansas City, to be assayed, not to Denver. Why? What was in Denver that caused him to avoid the place? Perhaps, it was who was in Denver. There still remained too many unanswered questions for him to make educated decisions.

'I ain't sure what to do, Grady. You have any suggestions?'

Grady nodded. 'Well, I reckon if I were callin' the shots, I'd head fer Denver an' have that quartz you got in yore pocket looked at. I reckon it'd help some to know fer shore what we're lookin' at.'

Caleb considered the suggestion — of course, Grady was right. So they mounted and rode back up the slope, where Grady waited on the rim and watched, while Caleb rode down into the basin. At the edge of the bluish clay deposit, where the occupants of the cabin had been digging, Caleb stepped down, pulled out an empty Arbuckle's sack, taken from one of Grady's packs, then dug into the clay with his knife, putting a sample of it inside the coffee sack. Then they rode from the box canyon, turning northeast toward Denver, and hopefully an answer to at least one of their questions.

16

South of Buena Vista, they turned down Trout Creek. Once out of the timbered-covered hills, they rode steadily east across the high mountain plain, until they came to the South Fork of the Platte River. Following the South Platte through the towering peaks east of the plain, then out on to the open prairie, they walked their mounts down the main street of Denver, five days after leaving the canyon where they had found the blue clay.

The sun was high overhead and the air around them was warm, as they stepped down at the hitching rail before the assayer's office, and loosened their cinches. With the Arbuckle's sack in hand, Caleb stepped through the door and walked up to the broad counter inside.

He was greeted by a round-faced,

jovial gent with red hair and bushy eyebrows over deep-set blue eyes that were framed by gold-rimmed spectacles. He was a friendly fellow, who seemed to have a perpetual smile on his broad face.

He slapped his hands together and rubbed them back and forth, as he cheerfully said, 'Good morning, gentlemen. What have you for me today?'

Caleb extended the hand holding the sack and placed the bag on the counter. When Charles Magee, the assayer, opened it and looked inside, his expression turned to one of utter surprise. He glared over his specs into the eyes of the young man facing him.

'Do you know what you have here, young man?'

Caleb shook his head. 'No, sir, that's what we came here to find out.'

The assayer nodded. 'I'm certain I know what this is, but give me a few minutes and I'll run a quick test on it. It won't take long,' and he disappeared through a door leading to a back room.

'What the devil you reckon we've found, son?' Grady asked nervously, as he lit his pipe.

Caleb had done much thinking, as they had traveled across the mountains from the valley, and believed he had been able to piece a few things together. But now he simply shook his head and placed his finger over his lips, urging Grady to remain silent for the time being. Soon Magee returned to the counter and handed the sack back to Caleb.

'Well, what you have in that sack is just what I thought it was. It's *kimberlite*.'

There was that word again. *Kimberlite*.

'Excuse my ignorance, mister,' Caleb said timidly, 'but just what is kimberlite?'

Unwilling to believe anyone would bring to him such a rare sample without knowing its significance, the assayer looked irritably from one man to the other.

With a degree of sarcasm and a definite edge to his voice, he gruffly said, '*Really*, gentlemen, I did my studies at Princeton College in New Jersey, Class of 1860, and graduated fourth in my class. I have held a position in the *State Department of the United States Government*, then applied for an opening within the Department of the Interior and moved here ten years ago, for the climate.

'Gentlemen, in the past ten years, I've assayed thousands of samples, and no one in that time has ever attempted to make me look foolish. I am an intelligent man, so please, *don't mock me*. Now, if that is all you need from me today, I'll bid you, 'Good day', gentlemen.'

Caleb looked at Grady, who was smiling around the stem of the pipe. The young gunman grinned back at the old prospector, then returned his attention to Magee.

'Whoa, pardner, pull in your horns. We ain't tryin' to poke fun at ya.

Neither of us has any idea what this *kimberlite* is. Let me back up a ways, so ya understand a bit about why we're here.'

He quickly filled the man in on all that had happened, his father sending the sample to Kansas City, his mother's letter to him, and finally of the murders and fire.

'A week or so back, I sent a telegraph message to Kansas City askin' for a copy of the report Dad got on the sample he'd sent. The fella at the assay office wrote back that his office had been broken into and reports had been stolen, includin' the report on Dad's samples.

'But the assayer included in his message that Dad's samples consisted of kimberlite. Now, I'll ask ya again. What the deuce is *kimberlite*?'

The assayer had been too quick to be insulted by this man's presumed mockery, and had just been put in his place. Now he was embarrassed.

'I apologize, young man. I truly

thought you were being facetious. Now, without going into a considerable amount of geology, I can tell you that *kimberlite*, which is also known as 'blue ground', is a dark colored igneous matter that originates from pockets deep within the earth, and contains many minerals within its structure.

'Seismic events — earthquakes if you will — occur causing fissures, or cracks, in the earth's mantle. Then, during volcanic events, magma is pushed up through these fissures. The magmatic intrusions solidify, forming what is known as 'pipes', then when a pocket of kimberlite, that lies along one of these pipes, is subjected to the super pressures from deep within the earth, it is pushed upward, through the fissures to the surface, usually ending in a depression or basin — a 'lake', as they are called.

'I could be quite technical and use numerous scientific terms, but I think I have explained it as simply as I possibly could. Without at least some knowledge of geology, I'm sure it is difficult for you to understand.

'But it is a significant process,' he quickly added, as he pointed his finger into the air to emphasize his statement, 'for *kimberlite* is best known as a means by which diamonds are brought to the earth's surface.'

Suddenly Grady's head snapped sharply around to face Caleb, who quickly flashed him a knowing glance. Caleb hoped the old man would not blurt out anything about the deposit of blue clay or the crystalline rock, which he kept in his pocket.

But the old man was a seasoned prospector, and not subject to betraying the whereabouts of an important find. Grady had no knowledge of the value of diamonds, only that they were considered the most valuable gem on earth, but when he remembered the leather bag under the blanket in the corner of the cabin, he realized there must be a small fortune in it.

'You know,' the assayer thoughtfully

added, 'there was a fellow in here, a couple of months back, with some ore samples he needed assayed. They didn't turn out to be much, only a smattering of gold in them, but while he was here, he mentioned something about kimberlite.

'He claimed he personally had not come across any, but he had heard of a man who had. Now what was that fellow's name? Hold on a minute, I've got a copy of that report on the ore he left with me. Give me just a moment, I'll see if I can find it.'

Magee once again turned from the counter, this time walking to a file cabinet in the corner. After a couple of minutes of sorting through his files, he came back with the report in question.

'Ater, was that fellow's name. Yes sir, Ellis Ater. You know him?'

'No, sir, I've never heard the name,' Caleb replied. 'You know him, Grady?'

'Nope. That handle don't ring no bells with me.'

Magee shook his head. 'Well, I hope

I've helped you, gentlemen. That kimberlite *is* a rare thing, but not *all* kimberlite deposits contain diamonds. However, if you ever come across one that does, the prospects can be unimaginable.'

Suddenly Caleb wanted to be away from the assayer's office, so he thanked Magee and led the way out the door. He had gotten the answer he sought, and what an answer it was. His dad had found the 'lake', as Magee had called it, and was looking for diamonds. Were the tiny stones in the bag diamonds? And who were the men living in the cabin?

'Grady, I've got to ask another favor of ya.'

The old prospector again smiled around the stem of his pipe. 'Let 'er rip, son. Like I said b'fore, I'll do whatever I can to help ya get to the bottom of all this.'

'We need to keep an eye on their diggin's, only I need to get back to Del Norte. That leaves you, if ya don't mind goin' it alone, to watch that canyon.

'I'll give ya the money to buy more grub, if ya don't mind goin' back there. I'd say ya oughta be able to follow that game trail, the one we's ridin' b'fore we came down off the mountain, on up to the top of the rim overlookin' that box canyon. Find a place up on top and just keep an eye on things; just watch those fellas. I'll get back up that way as soon as I can.

'For now, I'm gonna head for the railroad station. I'll hop the next train south and get off down at Walsenburg, then cut across the Sangre de Cristos for Del Norte. I've gotta ask around and see if anybody around there knows anythin' about that blue clay or those diamonds. Whether I get any answers or not, I'll ride back up to meet ya, then we'll pay those gents a visit.'

'I'll do whatever ya need did, Caleb. You just stay outta trouble, 'cause I won't be there to watch yore back 'round them cutthroats down to Del Norte.'

Caleb smiled at his old friend and

said, 'I'll be careful,' as he pulled another gold eagle from his pocket. He handed the coin to Grady, then they parted company, Grady heading off to purchase supplies, with Caleb bound for the depot.

Immediately after replenishing his supplies, Grady left town, bound for the hidden canyon located along the north face of Mount Ouray.

The next afternoon, Caleb boarded the southbound train; the roan was loaded into a cattle car. The day after that, he crossed over the Sangre de Cristo Mountains and again rode out on to the high plain. By noon of his third day from Walsenburg, he rode up to Aaron Johnson's livery and stepped down.

17

After stripping the gear from the roan, Caleb fed Red and ran a brush over him, while the big red horse ate. Johnson joined him as he saw to the animal.

'So, how'd he do, Caleb?'

'Good enough so that I'll buy him, if you'd part with him.'

Johnson smiled, happy that his horse had served his young friend well. 'First off, I'm shore glad he did good fer ya, son. As fer sellin' 'im to ya, if ya want 'im, he's your'n.

'Now I owed yore paw thirty dollars, from a deal we made a while back, so if'n you'll take the roan in payment, we'll call 'er even,' and he held out his hand.

Caleb smiled at the hostler and took the hand offered him. 'Done,' he said, and the deal was struck.

'I brung yore paint over from the hotel's barn,' Johnson stated as he pointed toward a stall in the far corner of the barn. 'He's a right fine pony, hisself.'

'Yeah, but he's a cowpony from down New Mexico way, and I've got no idea how he's gonna fare in these mountains. But that roan's a horse a fella can depend on in the high lonesome. That rascal took me over some country I's right timid to cross. But he never flinched — not once. I'm right proud to own him.'

With that, Caleb took a five dollar gold piece from his pocket and extended it toward Johnson. 'For the board of both animals, Aaron.'

'I'll not take a dime from ya, boy. Like I done told ya, you an' yore folks are good friends, an' I don't take pay from my friends.'

'Well, I don't impose on *my* friends, and grain ain't free, so I can't take 'No' for an answer. You'll shame me, hurt my feelings, if ya don't at least let me pay for the keep of my animals, Aaron. I mean it.'

So after giving it some thought, Johnson took the half eagle and nodded.

'Good,' Caleb said, as he placed the brush on a shelf. 'I appreciate it, my friend. Now, do ya have any coffee on?'

Johnson chuckled, then led the way into his quarters. Even after so many years of knowing Aaron Johnson, this was the first time Caleb had ever been inside the man's residence.

Surprisingly, it was a tidy little room with a bunk in the near left corner, an old armoire standing at its foot. A table and two chairs filled the corner on his right, and a small cook stove stood in the far right corner. No clothing lay about, as one might expect in an old bachelor's quarters.

Johnson pointed to the nearest chair, then quickly retrieved two cups and filled them with hot, strong, black coffee. Caleb liked his coffee strong, but when he took that initial swallow, he was nearly shocked to tears, for the brew was as bitter as quinine. Aaron Johnson, on the other hand, smacked his lips, then wiped them with his shirt sleeve.

'Aaahhh, man, that's good coffee,' the hostler stated proudly.

Caleb chuckled. 'Well, it'll sure keep a fella wide awake . . . and put a heavy growth of hair on his chest.'

After another swallow of the full-bodied beverage, Johnson asked, 'Now, son, yore a fella what looks like he's got a thang on 'is mind. What can I he'p ya with?'

Caleb needed to obtain as much information about his dad's activity as possible, but how much of what he already knew did he convey to Johnson? He decided he must simply play it by ear.

'Dad was exploring around up in the neighborhood of Marshall Pass. Did he ever confide in you about what he was lookin' for, or if he ever found whatever it was?'

Johnson gave the question quick consideration, then answered, 'He come in here one day, oh, it musta been nigh on to a couple of years ago, sayin' he needed to buy a couple of extry horses an' a pack animal. I owed 'im a considerable sum fer a loan he made me some time back, so I offered the animals in payment. He said I'd do no such thang, fer he didn't need the money, an' considered the loan a good inves'ment, jus' told me to pay it when I had it extry. We discussed it a might, but fin'lly he threatened to buy 'is stock somewheres else. So, I sold 'im a bay geldin' , a little dun mare and a ole Mizzura mule to pack 'is goods, a jack 'round eleven year ole.

'As I understand it, that were about the time he turned the runnin' of the ranch over to them Mexicans what worked fer 'im, an' went to takin' yore maw with 'im on 'is escapades into them hills. They lit outta here sometime durin' the wee-hours, takin' them horses and the mule with 'em.'

Now, Caleb became more confident that his dad had had good reason for searching that area north of the confluence of Poncho and Starvation Creeks. His gut was telling him that the canyon he and Grady had located was the same place his dad had found. Now, he had only to discover the identity of the man behind LaCrosse's killing of his parents, and his attempt to kill him, then he would look into whether or not his dad had registered a claim on that deposit of blue clay.

'Then a while after that,' Aaron went on, 'him an' yore maw come in, an' sent a parcel off to Kansas City. They never said what were in it, but I reckon folks in these parts has seen enough ore sent off fer assayin' to know what were in that box.

'After another little while, he got 'is re-port from the assayer. He never said nothin' to nobody, but him an' her was nowhere to be found that next mornin'. Come to find out, they'd bought their provisions from Conrad the night after that letter come, an' slipped off ag'in, when nobody were lookin' .

'*Well*, folks went to talkin' , an' I reckon all the gossips had plenty to hash over, fer a month or so. But, after a bit, the talk died down an' thangs got back to normal.

'Everthin' was quiet 'round here, 'til LaCrosse an' his outfit hit town. Nobody knowed anythin' about 'em. Didn't nobody fess up to hirin' 'em, nor have any idy how they's makin' their livin' , but they had plenty of money to spend. They jus' loaf 'round the Big Bear an' purty much stay outta trouble . . . 'til you come to town, anyways.'

Johnson gave Caleb a knowing look; Caleb simply shrugged and took another swallow of the black, repulsive liquid in his cup. He could not help but think, he liked his coffee strong, but this stuff was a far cry from just being strong.

'Them two ole boys,' Johnson continued, 'what got theirselfs all shot to blazes, was lookin' fer you, huh.'

Without waiting for an answer, he went on, saying, 'I ain't the sharpest tack in the box, son, but I notice thangs. Them boys skulked around watchin' ya ever' minute. I seen 'em more'n oncest.

'Ever' time you ambled 'round town, they's shadowin' ya, watchin' yore ever' move. I reckon they even seen ya come into town that first night, when ya conversed with ole Grady Bolton, over to the Rio.'

When Caleb's face showed his concern, Johnson added, 'Oh, it mighta been that confounded Charlie Gantz, what got the word 'round. He's the biggest dang gossip in this town. Can't nothin' go on, nor be said, in that blasted saloon of his'n, that don't finally make the rounds. Why, I'd bet my last nickel, yore bein' back in town was knowed, by most ever'body, by noon the next day.' He took another swallow from his cup, then added, 'But I wouldn't bet on him bein' the only one knowed you's here.'

Quickly thinking about that, Caleb

said, 'Somebody shot at me and Grady later that night, while we's settin' by our fire. Shot at us from about four hundred yards, with a big bore long gun. Got any ideas about that?'

Aaron Johnson was nodding excitedly. 'Somebody *borrowed* that chestnut out yonder in the corral, sometime durin' that night. Never heared 'im take 'er from the corral, but I did hear a rider leavin' town sometime after I went to bed. Didn't give it no thought, 'til I went out the next mornin' an' found out that horse'd been rode hard an' put up wet. Whoever took 'er, musta covered a lotta ground in a hurry.

'After I got over bein' mad, 'cause some yahoo'd took my horse without askin', I looked 'round some, an' found the fella's boot tracks. Them tracks showed a boot with flat heels, Caleb. Now I don't know who them boots b'long to, but I'd say he were a city gent, not one of them Texican cowboys.'

For more than two hours, Caleb and

Aaron Johnson talked and drank more of the black varnish remover Johnson called coffee. During that time, Caleb learned the names of those who had come to the neighborhood within the past two years. If someone other than Simon LaCrosse was behind this deal, it was likely one of those newcomers was the culprit.

Two of those men were ranchers, one a merchant, all family men with children. The only single man in the group of newcomers was the school teacher, Allen Snowden.

But Snowden had been sent for less than a year ago, to take the place of the recently departed Jerry Lawson, the man who had been master of the Del Norte School for eight years. But where had he come from? How did he know the town was in need of a new school master? Had it been a coincidence that he had applied to the mayor only two months before Lawson's demise? Maybe, but Caleb didn't believe in coincidences.

'Aaron, what do ya know about this Snowden gent?'

Johnson scratched his head, as he looked curiously into Caleb's eyes. 'Not much, I reckon. Come from back East, some'heres. Mostly stays to hisself, 'cept'n when they's one of them socials down at the church, Fourth of July, or at that Founder's Day shindig the mayor an' them folks puts on ever' year. Seems like a nice enough fella. Whatcha thinkin' , boy?'

'Oh, it's prob'lly nothin' ,' Caleb responded. 'I met him when I first got back to town, and you're right, he seems like a nice fella.' Then he sighed in his frustration, and added, 'I reckon I'm just graspin' at straws.'

It was almost suppertime when Caleb left Johnson. The sun was nearly down behind the peaks of the Divide, when he made his way between the buildings and down an alley to the edge of First Street, across from the hotel. There he stood in the shadows, surveying the street.

Things were already shaping up to be a lively ole night at the Big Bear Saloon. Men were drifting in from the street, and Homer Ludlow was already banging away at the keys on that old tinny piano. But on the porch outside the batwing doors, sat Dieter Metzger's brother, August, and another of LaCrosse's bunch, Rowdy Corns.

Caleb recognized Corns, although he did not know him personally. Whether Corns would pull on him at first sight, Caleb could not say, but as for August, he knew the answer to that.

August and Dieter had never been what one would consider 'loving' brothers, but blood is blood, and it's thicker than water, as they say. August would not allow the killing of his blood kin to go without reprisal. He would draw on Caleb immediately on sight, so Caleb knew he must avoid the Big Bear Saloon . . . for now.

Turning, he retraced his steps up the alley to Front Street, then turned left, walking the length of the street to the edge of town and around the last building. From where he stood, he could plainly see the Conrad house. A light showed through the window of the parlor, dimly illuminating a portion of the front porch.

Mrs Conrad would soon be setting supper on the table. Caleb debated with himself, whether or not to intrude upon their hospitality. Finally, he decided he would, for he needed to know more about the newcomers of which Aaron Johnson had spoken, and Conrad would certainly be the man to ask.

So he made his way along the buildings, quickly crossed over to the well-kept log house, then gave a soft tap on the door. When the door swung open, Lilly stood looking at him, quickly smiling and extending her hands, taking his in hers.

'Caleb! Come in, Caleb.' Then she turned and announced, 'Mother, Dad, Caleb is here.'

He could hear forks rattling against china as the elder Conrads rose from the table. Quickly, they entered the parlor.

'Come in, Caleb,' Russell Conrad invited. 'We were just sitting down to supper. Please, join us.'

'Thank you, Mr Conrad, but I just came over to have a talk with you. I've some questions you might be able to help me answer.'

'Well, I'll answer them if I can. You know I'll be glad to help you any way possible, but first, let's have our supper.' Then he turned to his wife. 'Mother, set another place at the table.'

So they ate. They were warm, friendly people, and they made him feel comfortable in their home. Suddenly he thought how much he would relish having the Conrads as in-laws. He smiled at the thought and looked across the table at Lilly, who was smiling back at him.

When the meal was over, he and Conrad retired to the parlor, sitting before the fireplace and smoking. Quickly, Caleb explained everything that had happened since his leaving Mexico. He told him of the ambush on the Llano Estacado, having been shot at while camped with Grady Bolton on Carnero Creek, and of his visit to Denver, which included finding the valley on Gray Creek.

Conrad nodded, when Caleb revealed this last detail. 'Caleb, when your dad brought in that first sample, he told me what he believed he had found. He gave me all of the geological jargon and explained how the blue clay is forced to the earth's surface.

'When the second sample went out, he told me it contained a small sample of diamonds. He wanted to have the stones analyzed, to see if they were worth his trouble. He never received the report for that sample, not from the blue clay, nor from the diamonds themselves.' Conrad hesitated, then added, 'I'm sorry, son. I should have told you all of this during your last visit. I felt badly for not saying anything, but I had hoped you would allow this thing to die down. I can see I was wrong to think so.'

At that, Caleb remembered the man's hesitation and caution when he answered his previous questions, during his earlier visit. But now, he pulled the small stone from his pocket and handed it to Conrad, who appeared to have no idea what he was holding.

'Is this a stone from that clay dirt?'

'It is. When Grady and I found that box canyon, we also found a cabin where two men are living, while they dig in that kimberlite deposit. In that cabin, we found a small bag containing a cupful of varying sizes of those stones.

'Grady should be back there, by now. He's gonna keep an eye on those fellas, until I can get a few more questions answered down here. Then I'll ride back up there and join him. When I get there, those fellas'll have to respond to any questions I don't already have the answer to, or pay the consequences.'

Conrad was shaking his head. 'Caleb, I knew your dad for a good many years, and we were the best of friends. So, I believe I can speak for him, when I say, don't go off seeking revenge for their deaths.

'Son, Angus was the most brilliant man I've ever known. His acquired education was simply the result of his brilliance, because his mind absorbed information like a sponge, and he remembered everything he ever read. I've never seen anyone like him.

'We spoke for hours, on numerous occasions, about his experiences in Persia and Egypt. I could listen to him for days on end, simply reminiscing about those places and the work he did there.

'He was my *best* friend and I miss him very much, Caleb. But I'd hate to see you get yourself killed trying to bring their killer to justice. I know your parents wouldn't want that either. They loved you very much, son, both your mother and your dad. He told me how much he loved and missed you.

'Why don't you just send a letter to

the US marshal's office in Denver? Explain everything to him, then let him take over.'

'I think that's already been done, Mr Conrad,' Caleb responded. Then he told him about the message received from the Kansas City assayer's office. 'So ya see, that marshal's probably already on his way here.'

'Good! Let him handle it.'

But Caleb wouldn't drop the subject. 'Mr Conrad, what can ya tell me about the folks who have come into the area in the past two years? I understand there's been a couple of ranchers, a storekeeper, and that school teacher.'

Conrad was exasperated. 'I thought you were going to wait for the marshal to get here.' But he could see Caleb was determined to continue with his own investigation, so, he shook his head and, reluctantly, gave him the information.

What he gave Caleb was basically the same details Aaron Johnson had given him. The ranchers were good, hard working, family men, who stayed on their ranches, except for their occasional trips to town for supplies.

The storekeeper appeared to be of the same type. No one in town knew anything about the man, other than he was from the East and married. He had done little business since coming to Del Norte, but those few customers he had had said he was friendly enough and dealt honestly. That was all anyone knew.

Then there was Allen Snowden. With the sudden loss of their school master, a committee was quickly appointed for the purpose of obtaining a replacement. During their first meeting, the mayor, who chaired the committee, presented them with a letter of application, which he had received two months earlier. Upon reviewing Snowden's impressive credentials, the committee voted unanimously to offer the position to him. The mayor immediately notified their new appointee by letter, and Snowden assumed the position one month later.

'That's about all I can tell you,

Caleb. All four men seem to be fine, upstanding citizens. I think you're looking in the wrong places, son.'

'Maybe, but it still remains to be determined who those two men in that valley on Gray Creek are. It looks like they're gonna be the key to this whole deal.'

Mrs Conrad and Lilly had joined them sometime during their conversation. Finally, Caleb looked into Lilly's eyes and smiled, suddenly forgetting the other reason he had come to their home.

Conrad and his wife left them there before the fire. For two more hours, they talked, Lilly telling Caleb of her desire to be his wife. She was being quite forward about the whole thing, but Caleb liked that about her, for she knew what she wanted and was willing to let her innermost desires be known to him.

Before he left, Lilly rousted her parents from their sleep and brought them back into the parlor. Standing beside the fireplace, sleepy-eyed and in their bed clothes, Caleb asked their permission to marry their daughter.

The Conrads were elated, giving their blessing immediately. Before Caleb left them, Lilly and her mother set a wedding date.

★   ★   ★

Back in his same hotel room, with a fire crackling in the small stove, Caleb stretched out on the bed, to consider what little he had learned from Aaron Johnson and his future father-in-law.

But that subject quickly took a back seat, for suddenly Lilly was the focus of his thoughts. In one month they would be married.

He would turn the investigation into his parent's murders over to the US marshal. After all, according to the wire he had received from Kansas City, the lawman would soon contact him.

Tomorrow, he would hire a man or two to help him, then they would ride to the ranch. He would build a new house, where he and Lilly would live. In the spring he would bring more cattle to the Rafter MC, and, in time, the herd would grow, along with their future.

Soon he fell asleep, Lilly paramount in his thoughts.

18

The sun had already been up for some time, when Caleb finished his breakfast. After a couple of extra cups of coffee, he left the hotel dining room and stepped through the front door, out on to the boardwalk. He took an empty chair, near the door, then with nimble fingers, rolled a smoke and put fire to it.

The town was busy, people going about their daily routines. Summer was over and the signs of fall were upon the landscape. The first snow of the season had come and gone, and the aspen leaves were turning to their brilliant gold, bringing a magnificent array of color to the countryside.

He loved these towering, jagged peaks, the low rolling foothills, and everything in between. How impulsive and immature he had been to have left them so abruptly.

And Lilly. He was young, yes, but how could he have not realized her feelings for him? Looking back now, he remembered things, little things she had said to him long ago, small clues to her feelings for him. He had been such a young fool.

But now that was all in the past. Now she was planning a wedding, preparing to be his bride. Now, he must find a man, or men, to assist him with the rebuilding of the Rafter MC ranch house.

So he came to his feet, ground out the butt of his smoke on his holster, and stepped into the street. Aaron Johnson would certainly know if there were any men in town, whom he could hire to assist with his building project.

With the thought of Lilly and their future foremost in his mind, he discounted the danger that for so long had threatened him, abandoning the caution with which he had previously walked the streets of Del Norte. No longer did he think of Simon LaCrosse and his cut-throats, not by design, but due to preoccupation.

But he arrived safely at Johnson's barn, where he obtained the names of two men the old hostler was certain would gladly work with him.

Johnson was also happy to hear Caleb was giving up his personal vendetta against those responsible for his parents' murders. He wholeheartedly agreed that, since the law was involved anyway, turning the matter over to the marshal was the best course of action, and the smartest thing Caleb had done since beginning his quest. Grudgingly, Caleb agreed.

After considering Johnson's comment, Caleb was suddenly questioning his decision to abandon his search. How could he have given up the investigation into his parents' death so easily? Was he losing his senses, all because Lilly had agreed to marry him? He was not the sort to relinquish his *duty*.

As he walked from the livery, headed for the Cantina Rio to locate the two men Johnson had named, he was torn between continuing his quest and turning the whole thing over to the marshal, who had not yet contacted him. Would the man ever show up?

After he located the two men, Randall Miller and Alistair Boggs, Caleb headed back to the hotel. Both men had agreed to work with him to build the new house. If Grady would also help, the four of them would be able to get the new structure in livable condition in only a couple of weeks.

Still thinking about building the new house, he had just stepped from the boardwalk on First Street, across from the Big Bear Saloon, when he noticed a lone rider sitting a tall blue roan, entering town from the east. He was watching the rider draw closer, when out of the corner of his eye, Caleb caught movement near the door of the Big Bear.

Quickly he was reminded of the

dangers he still faced. Turning his attention to the saloon doors, he found LaCrosse, August Metzger, Rowdy Corns, and Lee Cathcart looking in his direction, as they stepped into the street and proceeded to spread out. Without Caleb so much as looking again in his direction, the rider walked the roan past and stopped at the hitch rail in front of the hotel.

Now, LaCrosse and his bunch were evenly spread out across the street, more than an arm's length between them. Although he was faster than any two of these men, they were fast enough and all tough, and each man would take some killing.

Caleb, realizing his predicament, knew this was going to be touch and go. He would get bloodied up, but he would simply have to out last them.

'Ya got a lot a hard bark on ya, Kid,' Simon LaCrosse snarled. 'Yore dang shore a hard man to kill. But I reckon we can draw our pay, and leave these godforsaken mountains, after today, 'cause yore the last of the McConnells and you'll be dead shortly.'

Caleb hesitated to talk, as his eyes moved from one man to the next, up and down their line. Who would be the first to pull? Then he heard the grating of a boot heel, just behind him on his right.

'You've a friend, here, Kid,' a low voice, from his right, softly said. 'I'll take the two on the right, those two on your left are your pigeons. I've seen you shoot, so now this oughta be a fair fight.'

Caleb's mouth was dry, his insides churning. Never had he been so nervous before engaging in gunplay. Always before, he had entered a battle with little to lose, except for his own life.

But now he had Lilly, the prospect of restoring the ranch, and a future. And who was this stranger, who had so quickly volunteered to back him in his troubles?

'I wouldn't count my chickens b'fore

they're hatched, Simon. You boys might have a little more trouble pluckin' my feathers than you'd counted on.'

'You killed Dieter, Kid,' August interjected. 'I dang sure ain't gonna let ya slide on that.'

'That, my friend,' Caleb's mysterious companion quickly responded, 'was a fair fight. The Kid only had three guns facin' him then, and they drew first. I know, because I was there.'

Instantly Caleb's insides quieted.

Now he was ready. 'I don't reckon there's any sense in draggin' this thing out, LaCrosse. Y'all murdered my folks and their hired help, burned them alive. Now you're gonna pay for it. Fill your hands with iron.'

Fire darted from Caleb's Navy Colts, as a slug ripped through his shirt, opening a wound in his right side and causing him to slightly twist sideways. Both guns were hammering away, as he heard the continuous roar of the .45 Schofield bellowing near his right ear. Smoke filled the air, stinging his eyes and nostrils. Burning gunpowder flared on both sides of the cloud of smoke, as shot after shot was fired. Then, as suddenly as it had started, it was over.

LaCrosse was on the ground, the earth around him turning dark red with the blood that flowed from the three holes in his chest. Caleb's other target had been Rowdy Corns, who still stood before him, rocking back and forth with empty hands. Finally his knees buckled and he tipped backward on to the street, four freshly punched holes in the front of his plaid shirt, now stained crimson. August Metzger and Lee Cathcart lay sprawled side by side in the street, the guns near their outstretched fingers still smoking.

Caleb's head was spinning. He knew he had been wounded, but he stayed on his feet. He knew he had been hit twice, but not so hard. He was turning to see about his comrade, when he saw Lilly coming from the mercantile, her hands grasping her skirts, sprinting toward him.

Then from somewhere away from the street, another shot rang out, a heavy report echoing down the street, and Caleb was knocked sprawling to the ground. He lay face down in the street, and all the light about him instantly faded to blackness.

19

Caleb opened his eyes to find he was alone in a strange room, lying belly down on a bed. 'So, I lived through it, after all,' he muttered weakly. Then he closed his eyes and drifted off again.

When he again awakened, Lilly was in the chair beside him, reading a book.

'Lilly,' he whispered, 'where am I? What happened to the man who was with me?'

When she saw he was awake, Lilly burst into tears. 'Oh Caleb! I was afraid I'd lost you again. You have five wounds and you've lost a lot of blood. Lie still, until I get back, then I'll answer all of your questions,' and she quickly exited the room.

In only a few seconds, Lilly returned, followed by her mother and the man who had stood shoulder-to-shoulder with him on the street.

'Well, it's been said before, *amigo*, but I'll be glad to say it again. You're a hard man to kill, Sabinas Kid, and the Lord knows those fellas tried their dangdest.'

Caleb forced a weak smile. 'Roman, I surely was glad to see you. But what the deuce are you doin' in Del Norte . . . weren't you hit?'

Roman Bonner chuckled at his young friend. 'They must have all been shooting at you, my friend,' he answered, as he reached into his coat pocket and retrieved a US deputy marshal's badge.

'You rest easy, now. I'll stay around town until you're up and able to talk.' Roman pointed at Lilly and added, 'I just heard about your upcomin' weddin' . Looks like ya got yourself a mighty purty nurse, kid.'

Roman and Mrs Conrad went from the room. Lilly leaned forward and kissed Caleb on the cheek, then returned to her chair beside the bed.

'Rest easy, Caleb my love,' she whispered softly. 'I'll be here when you wake up.'

* * *

After five days of lying in bed, Caleb insisted he be helped to the front porch. There he was gingerly eased into a chair near the door and covered with a heavy blanket, his body and right leg wrapped tightly with bandages and his left arm immobilized in a sling. Lilly sat in the chair on one side of him, Roman on the other. He was still very weak, from the loss of blood from his five wounds, and his color resembled that of a man on his deathbed, but he wanted to be in the fresh air and refused to loiter one more day in that bed.

He had known about two of the wounds received in the gunfight with LaCrosse's bunch; when he received the other two, he had no idea. He had also been shot in the back with a big bore rifle.

But his assailant, shooting from an elevated position, had shot at such a steep angle the heavy slug failed to penetrate his body, glancing off of his shoulder blade, tearing through the heavy muscle of his back in a downward trajectory and exiting just above his left holster. It did, however, fracture his left shoulder blade . . . and had left a very nasty wound.

Finally, he was strong enough for Roman to fill in a few details for him, both of his being in Del Norte and of the gun battle in the street.

'When Isaac Samuels reported the break in at the assay office in Kansas City,' Roman began, 'I instructed him to notify me in case there were any inquiries that might pertain to the stolen reports. So, when you wired askin' about the report your dad had been sent, he came to me for instructions on how to respond.

'I told him to give you any details he might remember from the report, and to include in his wire that I would leave immediately for Del Norte. I'd have been here three days ago, but I rode the train up to Denver to visit that fella Magee, to see if anyone had

208

inquired about, or brought in any samples of, kimberlite.

'He told me that you had been in, and that he thought it queer that a young man, who knew nothing about what he had in that coffee sack, would bring in such a rare sample to be assayed.

'He also told me about the man, Ellis Ater, who had mentioned kimberlite, when he brought in an ore sample containin' such a small amount of gold. Magee thought it strange, because kimberlite is such a rare thing to find, and only someone with at least some knowledge of geology and diamonds would even mention it. He even suspected Ater's ore sample might have been 'salted', giving him an excuse for visiting the assay office . . . so he could ask about anyone finding kimberlite in the area. When Magee described this Ater, I knew right then he was the man I'd been looking for, for the past two years.'

Caleb gingerly shrugged. 'So who is

this Ater, and what the devil does he have to do with me?'

'Ellis Ater's real name is Julius Blankenbaker. He's also gone by the handle, Al Snow. But most recently, he's called himself, Allen Snowden.

'This Blankenbaker, or Snowden as you all know him, went to school in England, at Cambridge, where he studied geology and archeology under your dad.

'After coming to America, he finally ended up in St. Louis, where he worked for a mining outfit — the same company for which your dad had been a geologist. It almost seems like he followed your folks halfway around the world; for what reason, I can only guess.

'Well, this Blankenbaker was an accountant for that minin' outfit, and in the three years he kept their books, he embezzled over one hundred thousand dollars — a right tidy sum. By the time the theft was discovered, he was long gone.

'I don't know how he found out your folks were here, but evidently he learned your dad had sent in a sample of kimberlite. I have yet to discover how he got his information, but I'm gonna keep lookin' for his source, for a while anyway.'

'So this Snowden, or Blankenbaker, or whatever his name is, is the fella behind my folks' murders?'

'Yeah, it looks that way, Caleb. I've already found evidence here in town that connects him to LaCrosse.

'When he left St Louis, he headed south. That's what I was doin' down in Big Springs; I'd heard he was down in that neck-o'-the-woods. But my information was several months old, so by the time I got down there, he'd already left the country. Obviously, he was already up here.

'I can't account for his whereabouts during all of that period, the last two years I mean, but he did some travelin'. After hearing what I have about your former school teacher, I wouldn't be one bit surprised if Blankenbaker wasn't somehow responsible for his death, too, since he had applied for the position several months before the man's death. Otherwise, it would be one heck of a coincidence.

'As far as LaCrosse's outfit, Blankenbaker ran into them down around Fort Worth; I already told ya they were connected. I can only guess, but I think he musta talked Simon into buyin' in for a share of the diamonds. Only way I can figure it, now.'

'Well where the devil is Snowden now?' Caleb asked impatiently. 'Don't tell me the skunk got away, again.'

Roman laughed aloud at his young friend's fire. 'No pardner, he didn't get away. It was him that shot ya from the hotel window. When I heard that shot from up above and saw you go down, I pulled my belt gun and emptied it into that open window. When I got up there, I found Blankenbaker, or Snowden, dead on the floor, with a Spencer .56 layin' next to him. He ain't gonna bother anybody, ever again.'

As Roman completed his recap of his investigation, movement caught Caleb's eye. A half mile off to the northwest, he saw three riders coming toward town, over the open plain, one of them trailing a pack-animal.

As they neared the Conrad home, one of the riders threw his hand in the air and waved violently. When he was close enough for Caleb to hear him, he was yelling, 'Hah Caleb, looky here what I done found!' Caleb recognized the voice. It was Grady Bolton.

Caleb could still only vaguely make out the figures of the riders, but Lilly suddenly gasped and burst into tears. When the three drew up at the hitch rail, Caleb doubted his eyes, thinking he must be delirious.

When they stepped on to the porch, Abigail and Angus McConnell rushed to the side of their son, hugging and kissing him as though he had returned from the dead. Lilly continued to weep with joy. When Angus McConnell regained his composure, he told them what he knew, and explained where they had been.

Abigail had been traveling with her husband, but Caleb already knew that. On one of their returns to the ranch, they had found the houses burned and the Urbanias dead.

Angus at once became suspicious that someone had intentionally burned the cabins, thinking they had killed him and his wife, along with the Urbanias. So in an effort to convince the culprits all four were dead, Angus and Abigail had buried their friends, then made two more graves, hoping that if the arsonists returned, they would believe some passerby had found four burned bodies and buried them.

Since then, they had been living in the cabin on Gray Creek and working the kimberlite deposit, occasionally leaving the valley to travel to Gunnison, to obtain their supplies, and to hunt.

When Grady, who was watching from the bluff above the box canyon, realized who the two people working the kimberlite were, he rode down at once. He quickly explained to Angus and Abigail that Caleb had returned and was looking for their killers, and that he intended to kill everyone responsible. Upon hearing that, the three had left the canyon and ridden straight to Del Norte.

As the reunion wound down, Caleb introduced Roman to his parents, who told them the entire tale, from the day he had found their son near the waterhole on the Llano, to the gunfight on First Street.

When his mother mentioned caring for him, while he recovered from his injuries, Caleb shook his head.

'I'm fine here, Mom. I'm stayin' with Lilly in her room, while I'm recoverin' .'

'Caleb!' Mrs McConnell gasped.

For the first time since the gunfight, Caleb felt like laughing, although it cost him dearly, pain stabbing at his back, shoulder, and sides.

'It's OK, Mom. She's been lookin'

after me and sleepin' in a chair next to the bed. But I figured I oughta make an 'honest woman' of her, anyway, so we had the mayor come by yesterday.

'Folks, meet your new daughter.'

Author's Notes

Llano Estacado
(aka: The Staked Plains): The vast mesa, commonly known as the 'Llano', is the region in the southwestern United States which lies at the southern end of the High Plains section of the Great Plains of North America. It encompasses parts of eastern New Mexico and north-western Texas, including parts of the Texas Panhandle. One of the largest mesas on the North American continent, the elevation rises almost uniformly, at a rate of 10 feet per mile, from 3,000 feet in the southeast to over 5,000 feet in the northwest. With the terrain lying in such a gradual slope, the elevation change is indistinguishable, so travelers perceive it as being flat. The Llano is bordered on the north by the Canadian River, and on the east by the sheer cliffs of the Caprock Escarpment (about 300

feet high) that lies between the Llano and the Permian Basin of West Texas. The Mescalero Escarpment towers over the edge of the Pecos River valley, serving as the Llano's western boundary. The Llano Estacado has no natural southern boundary, naturally blending into the Edwards Plateau near Big Spring, Texas. The Llano stretches approximately 250 miles north to south, 150 miles east to west, encompassing some 37,500 square miles, an area larger than all of New England. It covers all or part of four counties in New Mexico and thirty-three in Texas.

Playas: are small, shallow, temporary bodies of water with gradually sloping sides and clay soil bottoms. Thousands of playas (96 per cent of all playas in the world) literally dot the Llano.

Kimberlite (aka: Blue Ground): is a dark-colored, heavy, often altered and fragmented, intrusive igneous rock that contains diamonds in its rock matrix.

Kimberlite, along with a similar rock called lamproite, is important for delivering diamonds to the crust through magmatic intrusions that solidify into pipe-like structures. Kimberlite 'pipes' are rare around the world. True to this story, **Kimberlite deposits have been discovered in the northern regions of Colorado**.

Diamonds: are formed at high pressure and temperature in the Earth's mantle at a depth of at least eighty-seven miles below the earth's surface. True to this story, **Diamonds have indeed been found in northern Colorado**.

We do hope that you have enjoyed reading this large print book.

Did you know that all of our titles are available for purchase?

We publish a wide range of high quality large print books including:
Romances, Mysteries, Classics
General Fiction
Non Fiction and Westerns

Special interest titles available in large print are:
The Little Oxford Dictionary
Music Book, Song Book
Hymn Book, Service Book

Also available from us courtesy of Oxford University Press:
Young Readers' Dictionary
(large print edition)
Young Readers' Thesaurus
(large print edition)

For further information or a free brochure, please contact us at:
Ulverscroft Large Print Books Ltd.,
The Green, Bradgate Road, Anstey,
Leicester, LE7 7FU, England.
Tel: (00 44) **0116 236 4325**
Fax: (00 44) **0116 234 0205**

THE DEVIL'S PAYROLL

Paul Green

When bounty hunter John Harrison captures fugitive outlaw Clay Barton, he's persuaded by Maggie Sloane to allow the captive to lead them to the loot robbed from an army payroll. But Barton double-crosses them and the mysterious Leo Gabriel kidnaps Maggie. With a veteran Buffalo Soldier, Sergeant Eli Johnson, at his side, Harrison battles ruthless vaqueros and a Comanche war party to recover the money, re-capture Barton and rescue Maggie . . . but a surprise awaits him when he finally catches up with his enemies . . .

HELL ON HOOFS

Lance Howard

Arriving in Lancerville, John Laramie hoped to escape his old life as a man-hunter and settle down. But there he finds he's torn between the demons of his past and hope for a brighter future when a young woman seeks his help in getting rid of a vicious outlaw. Then the Cross Gang attacks him and the young woman's life is put in danger. But will it cost Laramie more to win than to lose in a deadly showdown?

TROUBLE AT MESQUITE FLATS

Will Keen

Arriving in Mesquite Flats, ex-New York businessman Bodene Rich is committed to Yuma Penitentiary for a vicious assault. He's released, in light of new evidence, and pardoned by Warden Bradley Shaw. On the day of Rich's release, Shaw resigns, but an unknown gunman then shoots him dead on the trail. Rich once again is in trouble. And, in a showdown, he's embroiled in a bloody gun battle, where the outcome hangs in the balance until the final shot . . .